Saint Patrick

13 Doses of Laugh

Othniel Poole

Strategic Book Publishing and Rights Co.

Copyright © 2020 Othniel Poole. All rights reserved.

No part of this book may be reproduced or transmitted in any form or by any means, graphic, electronic, or mechanical, including photocopying, recording, taping, or by any information storage retrieval system, without the permission, in writing, of the publisher. For more information, send an email to support@sbpra.net, Attention: Subsidiary Rights.

Strategic Book Publishing and Rights Co., LLC
USA | Singapore
www.sbpra.net

For information about special discounts for bulk purchases, please contact Strategic Book Publishing and Rights Co., LLC. Special Sales, at bookorder@sbpra.net.

ISBN: 978-1-952269-23-3

Green Paul Tie

23rd December 2019;
25th January 2020

Here I am, psychiatrist/actor Patrick Curlewis;

Father of many rations, that is to say:

Sensible children with faith who feed the world.

My wife is Leah Curlewis, a shapeshifting woman who can go back in time and be in multiple places at the same, which I'd say makes a change from my exes; the issue mainly being that they were all her.

She decided that I should be a deacon, and be the bishop of one princess; and though merry I felt united to my grief that she had deceived me.

But all things bear fruit for those who Love God. Whenever she changes her face, we have a child. But most of the time, when we are alone, she has a face reserved just for me, Jesus and the church. A most radiant face if I may have such ideals; and I will not change them; and it only takes me to say.

I am travelling back to Rome to answer the big question, what was the glorious Paul (in the words of Polycarp) like?

I find a very tarrying, numb, shivering, stammering man, weeping and gnashing his teeth, rattling his crimson chains and calling out with crusty green and greys grimy temples and rags like an autumn gorse; I was suprised, but I tried not to hold a grudge.

He has a bowl of red water, and a stale stone loaf of bread.

"Would you like some lavender water?" I asked the metaphyiscal Tarsun.

I splashed some on his chin and he calmed down a bit.

"You may be small in the eyes of Romans," I said, "but you have a very big heart and a very big brain and very big love for the people of Europe, Paulo mine."

The marriage chains of death leave him, and Paul and I leave the prison in Rome.

I, Patrick leads him step by step, like tiptoe through the tulips, with literary and folky yellow tulips, through Gaul and Nice, detouring through Galilee and spice, making a full 180, until we read the Pyrenees.

And read the writing here:

Happy birthday, Saul of Tarsus.

And Paul weeps for joy, and he is presented with a bride who has been waiting like a patient in a cafe:

Kempa Apocalynta!

She is dressed in white and with a big blue wedding ring with a silver crystal.

And I, Patrick, as priest, Irish Catholic, read the liturgy that was prophecy for it had not been written in this day, and Paul kisses his bride passionately and weeps so much and he feels okay and abounds in prayers.

And Saint Saul Neoking as he is now called writes thousands of books in his first 40 years of marriage. How to make tents, how to make candles, be a centurion, be a bathouse owner, be a preacher, be a husband, in detail, love songs, songs about nature, songs about raising children with the detail of a mother, he writes church history in the style of Kings and Chronicles, he writes fiction for children, and lengthy genealogies, he writes about fashion and sport and how to make armour, he writes scripts for people to play out, he writes how to speak in code. He writes out the dictionary of heavenly languages, and he is fully satisfied, and he goes with I, Patrick, my wife, Leah, my twin sister Jane and all of their children through time, heralding the end of every age, and the marriage of every man to one woman.

Saint Patrick The One One (11) Loved

6th November 2019 - 25th December 2019

Contents:

1: Pierced

2: Messy

3: Maggie

4: Jodie

5: Sledge

1: Pierced

6th November 2019

Lemuel Goldstein got me in his office, me and Leah, my wife. Leah was herself, herself, so I guess the old Hebrew she considered to be part of the family. Which was so good, I love her for that, accepting that she can be herself with more than just me.

"I've got a Christian film pitch for you, Patrick Curlewis," said Lemuel, "and it's full gospel."

"Well, full gospel goes down bittersweet," I said, "what do you have in mind, Godly Goldie?"

"We'll call it *Pierced*," said Lemuel, "and it will be about Jesus Christ of Nazareth, particularly about his interactions with prostitutes."

"Yes, he loved all women," said Leah, "more than any man who has ever lived."

"Even more than Solomon," said Lemuel, "so they say. They also say the Emperor has no clothes, and that lilies wore more than the King of Israel. But I'm being cheeky to you..."

"So what does he say to these women of the night?" I asked.

"Well, he is very interested in their flow of blood," said Lemuel, smiling, "because he would bleed for all."

"You might offend a few people," I said.

2: Messy

Christmas Morning 5780

We were walking in the dark, me and Leah, from the film set in LA. We were walking past endless McDonaldses. I think I even saw a KFC! They had popcorn chicken with fairly floss in it!

"Are you sure you want to do this?" she said. "Like, I know when we work we've got to serve people who don't believe what we believe. That happens. Muslims work for Hindus to provide for their Muslim family. Mormons work for Catholics. This sort of thing happens all the time."

"Lemuel," I said, "he's made us do some weird cafonkey before. Remember *A Woman For Woman's Sake*?"

"All too well, hun," said Leah, "now, why don't we beat this Jew at his own game?"

"Pardon?"

"We'll get Jesus Christ, our Lord and Saviour, to play you playing Jesus," she said. "He likes acting, remember the road to Emmaus in the Gospel of Luke 24."

"What 24?" I said, checking my watch.

And so we walked, and time went backwards, and we made our way to a carpenter shop in Nazareth where Joseph Ben Jacob Ben Matthan, in his khaki coloured dreamcoat, was teaching an 11 year old Jesus to hammer a nail.

"Just pretend it's a statue of Zeus in the Temple," said Joseph to his ward, "and then I'll give you presents for a week."

"I love presents," said the Child, "I love when people love me and ask me to do things, I love people so much, Daddy. I know you're away a lot and people ask where you are, but I don't mind. I'm not like Syd Barrett or Roger Waterstein in Pink Floyd."

"Pardon?" said Joseph Ben Jacob, looking flummoxed.

"Hey Patrick," said Jesus, and ran to give me a hug round the knees, "you are doing so well as a psychiatrist. You're like Doctor Who with a blister pack full of ecclesiastic ecstasy."

"How do you know so many big words when they won't let you in the synagogue?" asked Joseph.

"Why won't they let Yessie into the synagogue?" asked Leah.

"He glows in the dark," said Joseph, "they don't comprehend it."

"I'm like a yoyo," said Jesus, "they'll end up hiding me in the garden from the government."

"You'll always be here in my head, boyo," said Joseph, and kissed Jesus on the forehead.

"Yessie," I said, getting down on his humble level.

"Yeah, Paddy Boom Boom?"

"One of your family wants to make a movie about you in the year 2020, that everyone will see."

"Do they?" Jesus clapped his hands, "I love movies! My favourite one at the moment is Frankenstein!"

"What do they teach them in these schools?" said the dreamer with the hammer.

"So what do you think?" I asked Jesus, "How would you like us to make the movie of your life?"

"Um..."

"They want it to be about the way of women," said Leah.

"Oh ok," said Jesus, "be careful, you don't want to lie about it."

He ran up and got his hammer.

"Look, I love women a lot," he said, "I believe I can come up with a solution. Let me play my adult self as me the child playing you playing the adult me, and we'll go and meet Lemmie Bullion McDooglepants and we'll make his movie."

"I love you, Jesus," said Leah.

I took Jesus by the hand and led him across the tachyon zebra crossing.

"Notice the left and right as you cross," I said.

"But don't let either know what the other is doing, silly billy Paddy Boom Boom McWeaselbeans." said Jesus.

Soon we were at the film set. Without a script. Oh boy!

3: Maggie

25th December 2019

Jesus had given the changeling gene to all the cast of *Pierced*, and now they were all 11 and 12 year olds, except for Lemuel, Leah and me. I had a shaved head and so did Jesus, he stood beside me.

"Child is the father of the man," said Jesus, "I'll tell Brian that."

He looked up at me and smiled.

"I know what to do," He said.

He pointed to a girl with thick wavy brown hair and a smile that reminded one of grunge, Mall Rats and a gentleness, a sensitivity and a hidden pain.

"Who is that?" I asked Child.

"That's the child actress Jodie Tulk," said Jesus, "she's had a very hard life and is not playing with a full deck. It's not her fault. The world needs at least one more Ace to be on your side."

"So you want her to be in the movie, bubula?" Lemuel gasped.

"Yes, sir," said Jesus.

Jesus walked over to Jodie and took her by the hand.

"Come follow me, sis," he said, "I'll make you a star, and you'll have lots of friends, and you'll be happy. I'll keep you away from bad drugs like meth, and you'll be able to have a drink once in a while and not go overboard. You'll have good guardians, and you won't have an affair with older men that you'll be writing songs about for the next 33 years. You'll run rehabs and sing songs for sick children. You'll have great Christmases, and some people will make fun of you, but listen... they make fun of Bono too. And he learns from it, you know? Everyone's a bit of a silly willy sometimes. Do you want to do a project with me, sis Jodie?"

"You talk a lot," said Jodie, after a pause.

"You'll do the talking in this one," said Jesus, and gently led Jodie in front of the camera.

And we dressed her in rags, stained rags. Rags stained red with dirt and grass stains and white paint. Her and Jesus were in the Judean city.

"Pierced," said Lemuel softly, "take one."

"And action," I said.

"Your line," Leah hissed to Miss Tulk.

"Gello," said Jodie, but we kept rolling, "do you like me?"

"Of course I like you," Yessue said, "you are a great person, and I think your father is really proud of you."

"Where is my Father?" said Jodie.

"If you've seen me, I can show you," said Jesus.

"What's your name?"

"Jes," said Messiah, "and yours?"

"Miriam Magdalene," said Jodie, "they call me Magdalene because I am maudlin sometimes."

"Why do you get sad?"

Jodie shied away, Jes caught her by the hem of her garment.

Jesus paused, and his face was screwed up like a fig that's been held on to too tight.

"I want to do a Waiter from The Hunted Planet," said Jesus, looking into the camera, "kiddies and those weak in the faith, do not keep reading. Patrick Curlewis does not want to hurt those weak in the faith by the books that he eats. But at the same time he wants to make movies, and I love him so."

Lemuel walked toward Jesus.

"What are you doing?" Lemuel said, "You're supposed to ask her about her way of women."

"I'm 11 years old, you creep," said Jesus, "what's wrong with you?"

Lemuel was taken aback.

Jesus produced the hammer from under his robe.

"You hypocrite, Lemuel Goldstein," Jesus said, clenching his teeth, "you have all this money to make movies but you don't help the mental patients by putting them in movies. You make Patrick do ridiculous things with his wife and put cameras everywhere. You read Torah and do anagrams for plots of movies, yet you do not share this talent nor believe the Bible you read. How will you be spared from my hammer?"

Jesus went to bop Lemuel on the knee, but Lemuel grabbed it in a rage. He pulled on it, and Jesus tried to wrestle it back.

"That's enough," I said, and gave Jesus back his tool from the old man.

"Bless you, Mr Director," said Jesus to Lemuel, "but don't ask me to stare at your back or anywhere else."

4:Jodie

25th December 2019

Jodie Tulk ran off crying and Jesus ran after her.

"What's wrong?" said Jesus.

"That was awful," said Jodie, "you're a Jewish boy and you got angry at a Jewish man. Family need to be at peace."

"He was going to make you do horrible things," said Jesus, "he doesn't represent Jews or Rabbis, he is himself. He is an individual, as Brian says."

"But you gotta serve somebody," said Jodie, "even you serve your two fathers."

Jesus put the hammer on a prop of a carpenter shop. There was sawdust on the bench, and he wrote something in the sawdust with his finger, then stood back up and spoke again to Jodie.

"Lemuel is not an Israel, but an Edom," said Jesus, "he is red. He is working for Manfred Eastern! I tell you the truth, we are in times of great division. That is good when you are in a cell and medicated with the truth of the womb, but in the world, it leads to a cracked egg. And that's no, yolk!"

"This isn't easy," said Jodie, "life isn't easy."

"Shall we tell Patrick about this?" said Jesus.

Jodie bit her lip.

"Why are you asking my opinion?" she asked.

Jesus took Jodie's trembling hand.

"Because I love you," he said, "even before you were born, Jodie Tulk, I have loved you. I loved you when your mother tried to make you what she never was. I was with you when you tried those strange pills and all that booze. I was with you when you sung very high in the paediatric psych ward those Seventh Day Adventists hymns that were obsessed with warding off secret societies. I was with you, and now here I am. Your best friend."

"My... best... friend?" said Jodie, a tear with a rainbow like an emerald going down her frozen cheek.

"Yeah," Jesus smiled, "I've got bags of time. From ages 12 to 30 I've got nothing booked."

He opened a New Testament in his robe to the gospels. It was empty for 18 pages in the early middle of the Gospel of Luke.

"See? I can spend 18 years with you. Just with you Jodie. I love you so much. I leave the billions and billions of people to go after the one. And I have found you, Jodie Tulk."

Jodie fell on the boy Jesus, and Jesus held her as she sobbed and sobbed and sobbed.

"You're okay," said Jesus, "you just fell over. People do that, especially when they're young. We're going to have some fun, okay?"

"Sometimes I feel so bad when I'm going through..." she hesitated, "you know..."

"I can show you how to deal with it," said Jesus, "and I learn from the things I suffer, so if you get angry at me, or throw something at me, or speed angrily in your car, or slap me, or knee me in the middle, I'll be ready to bear the world's burdens. It starts with one..."

"I love Linkin Park," said Jodie.

"If Patrick hurries up and discovers time travel, we'll get Chester back," said Jesus, "but for now, let's have fun. Do you like curry and lemonade with rice pudding for dessert?"

"Would you really eat a combination like that?" giggled Jodie.

"We'll put a green parasol in the lemonade, and a mint leaf on top of the curry, and a bit of honey on the rice pudding."

Jesus held Jodie's hand.

"Things go better when they go with things," he said, "like mayonaisse and tomato sauce."

"Is that a fact?"

"Well... sometimes chefs have to have a go," said Jesus.

And then He looked at you through this book.

"and my interpretation of that sentence is the only one. Derfla!"

5: Sledge

25th December 2019

Me and Leah were walking through the empty film set.

"Well, I guess we worked over Christmas and lost a day with the kids and didn't even get paid for the work we did." said Leah, "that's a bit of a caetheter mourn pie."

I noticed the hammer on the dusty carpenter bench. I gingerly picked it up.

"I think Fiona is going to ballet recital tomorrow," said Leah, "we can get Jane to babysit, but she's teaching Currer to be a good big brother. You've got to delegate to a family, and give the eldest responsibilities so he knows how to handle that double portion God gave him."

She whacked me on the shoulder.

"Are you listening to me, Patrick Curlewis?"

I motioned to what Jesus had written in the sawdust.

"Dear Paddy Boom Boom:

This is your sledgehammer. This is your testimony. Shed your skin. I will reward you with ten cities right now on Earth if you do what I command you. Lemuel Goldstein has defected to Manfred Eastern. He is going to do a b-movie about a cyborg called The Apotheosis of Gina Messyburger, and to film it they're going to make the robot version of Jane Eastern."

"The false prophet!" I gasped.

I kept reading the sawdust finger note:

You and Leah must split from Jane. She is in danger with you and you are in danger with her. She will go underground to the land of the fairies. That's elves, not Gary Russell land. She will send you correspondence by mole in the hole. When the mole in the hole emerges with bowl, then you will save soul and then eat a roll, and then the mole roll will have a portrait of a foal and then you will know that the Whore of Babylon is coming, because she is of horse.

And now, Paddy, I want you to take a new role. You are to become MAGNETO ALBO BURNS, and run for the Tupperware Party as Viceroy of Queen Jessica Mauboy. Find Jessica and she will then search for Jane Eastern to learn how to become a competent monarch. When this is done, Jane and Jessica can reunite with you, and you can take on Manfred for the first time. He will be knocked out by a deadly head wound. While he is dead, flee to Parahrabah and take a holiday for a bit. Jessica will stay in Australia and run the country, raise living standards for the Indigenous people and increase the compilation of languages, that all speech may be sanctified and made good. Zephaniah the prophet said that in the end we will all speak a pure speech. When she has done this, Manfred will rise once more. And he will be pierced with a scar, right eye darkened and right arm limp. And he will make his advocates do the same thing. He who has ears let him hear.

It was a big table.

TO BE CONTINUED IN ANOTHER SAINT PATRICK STORY...

25th December 2019

6:47AM

St Patrick Runs The Race

26th December 2019 - 30th December 2019

Contents:

Chapter 1: Eerie Cody Brown

Chapter 2: Trojan Force

Chapter 3: The Unforgivable Indulgence

Chapter 4: The Seven Names of David

Chapter 1:
Eerie Cody Brown

26th December 2019

Like a rainbow in an onion, Cody Brown was walking through the psych ward to a big red, hairy man with a stethescope.

Cody was dressed in a suit made of feathers.

"Manfred Eastern," said Cody, bowing and kissing the hairy man's wedding ring, "I have news of Patrick Curlewis."

"He is seen everywhere," said Manfred, "but what do you know?"

"I know that he is in gumboots," said Cody, "he is gardening on Parahrabah with his kids."

"I know just the thing to stop him," said Manfred, cracking his knuckles and then cracking crackers with the palms of his hands and spreading them all over the floor and then brushing the crumbs into the carpet of the psych ward with his feet.

"What is the thing that will stop an astropsychiatrist?"

"I will send my son," said Manfred, "the Son of Man."

"Who? The Lord Christ?"

"Naw," said Manfred, "London Eastern!"

He whistled, and a small child with yellow eyes, bright red skin and horns all over him came running up.

"Are you a visitor or a patient?" said Cody to the child.

"It takes a long time to grow up," said London.

Chapter 2:
Trojan Force

26th December 2019

And then there I was, on Parahrabah, with my parasol and my Paramore records. And there were butterflies everywhere, and the wind was the colour of Pocohontas.

"Paddy Boom Boom!"

It was Leah, my wife, with her everyday face she now shared with everyone because we were not ashamed. Not on Parahrabah, and not anywhere, because Parahrabah was on TV in the show *Physiognomy*. And everybody could see how ridiculous I was.

Leah was beautiful, she was never ridiculous. And if anyone makes fun of her, I'll have to call you. Ring, ring! Ring, ring! Shine on you crazy diamond, see the knees of the waxworks and say hello.

Ahem.

"We've still got Forrest Deacon as our director," said Leah, "but our producer is a dark horse known as Harrison Capone. He's always wearing sunglasses to bed."

"I don't mean to be a non-apple computer, especially on an Eden like this," I said, "but what nationality is Harrison?"

"I think he's from British India," said Leah.

"Do we get to meet him?"

At that moment, nine boys came running up to us. They had curly auburn hair and ruddy faces and were all carrying $50 notes from Australia.

"My boys!" cried Leah, and cuddled up to them and made funny faces and brought them deep into the family.

These were our new songs, our new sons: David, David, David, David, David, Davis, David, David and Dave.

You see, Leah had been trying on new bodies for a Brownlow Medal Ceremony. She didn't know any footballers, but she thought she could sneak us both in if I came in transmogrified as a football and could pose as my wife, which she really is, but in real life she doesn't kick me around to get her goals when she's been getting points.

Trouble was, the Brownlow ceremony had been filled with zombies. I didn't even know they were real.

"Brian's, Brian's," they said, because they couldn't spell and didn't believe in Jesus.

But I believe in Jesus. He was standing by the Tree of Furious, and he was shaking his head at me.

"Why did you do it, Patrick?" He said.

"What did I go?" I asked.

"Don't be preening what is dirty, Patrick." He said, "You made revelation cheap and named nine precious children all the same thing."

"It's a good name," I said.

"It's a name for a Dux, yes," Yeshua said, "But you don't find precious names for my little ones off currency. People don't name their children Stockmarkette and Lifeinsurance. The love of money is the root of all evil."

"Yes, and I have been experiencing a lot of success lately," I said, hanging my head.

"We don't read tabloids here on Parahrabah," said Jesus, "you don't need to gossip in a true family. Everyone knows everything about each other."

"We get it," said Leah, putting her hand on my shoulder.

"I'm just giving you the head's up," said Jesus, "Manfred Eastern is sending his son London to come and play with all your Davids. It's going to take him a while to get here by rocket ship, and before he does I want you to do something for me, so that you are not deceived and keep a clean face. Saving face is good, because then you have more face to face when facing recreational moments."

"Yes, you can't put all your face into the public arena," said Leah.

"So what do you want us to do?" I asked the Master, and Jesus smiled.

"I want you to give them all new names, so they can be real child-like emperors."

"How much time do we have?" I gasped.

Jesus smiled.

"Prophecy is pattern," He said, "you have six days, and then you can play pool on the seventh."

Chapter 3

The Unforgivable Indulgence

29th December 2019

Meanwhile Manfred Eastern was giving a speech in Kentucky to a bunch of frightened acid casualties.

"The Bible," he said, "let's read the Word. The Word is on the street. The Word is in the gutter. The Word is in the sink. The Word bin ein berliner. The Word is like a war with ads. So let's advertise. Lets make our tassels long, and our crosses huge. Let's post on social media what we are doing. Let's live stream and spend a lot of time getting ready before we spread the word. Let's cross the streams, let's put Jizya... I mean, Jesus, first."

The acid casualties shuddered, some cried, some screamed as if possessed by demons.

"Now, the Gospel of Matthew says that he who blasphem's the Holy Spirit will never be four-given. Now four in... Eastern cultures means the number of death. Si in Mandarin and Shi in Japanese. And look see? I am Eastern, and I am running for office against Dr Patrick Curlewis. Do you really want a *psychiatrist* telling you acid casualties how to live? You know what he's going to do? He's going to make you PhDs and theologians! No... we can be free of books. Follow the Word and be free of books."

"What is the Word?" said one tragic.

"Where can I speak this Word?" said another.

"Let me finish," said Manfred, putting his hand to his hip like Thom Yorke in the *Radiohead* video *Just*, "I told you the greatest commanment of all. He who blasphemes the Holy Spirit will never be four-given. Death, four, *si*, *shi*. He who says a Word against the

Holy Spirit will never be Death Given. So all we need to do for eternal life isn't baptisms or pish posh, but we need to say a word against the Holy Spirit."

"Who is this Holy Spirit that I may blaspheme him?" said a little man with scruffy short brown hair.

"He is what gives Patrick Curlewis his eloquence, his children and his romance, his career and his joy and his peace, his wealth and his stardom and mystical experiences. It gives him access to all he needs to do his work. *And that includes the opiates that oppress you!*"

The acid casualties began to boo and throw popcorn and soggy chips.

"So do you want to go all the way with me?" Manfred said, beckoning with his wriggling fingers. "Simple. ABCs. Normal stuff. Simply say "four", the number of si and shi."

The acid casualties hesitated, and there was an awkward silence.

"C'mon!" Manfred yelled. "C'mon."

And there was a teenager with long blonde hair and a haphazard moustache in the front. He came to the front. And he smiled and gave a salute to Manfred like Rimmer out of *Red Dwarf*.

"What's your name, brother?" asked Manfred.

"Battery Rachelson," said the youth.

Manfred thought long and hard about this, but then dismissed it.

"So, you will be the first to say Four and blaspheme the Holy Spirit and be saved?"

"F.... f... f..."

Manfred grinned a wicked dream, like Sleeping Beauty was going to dream smiles for 1000 years.

"F... f... f... f.. f.. ffffffff..."

And then God came and confused the language of good ol' Battery Rachelson.

"FIVE! FIVE! FIVE!"

And the rest of the LSD knockouts began to chant.

"GIVE! GIVE! GIVE!"

"Give to the poor," said Battery, "give to the burnout, give to the child, give to the desperate, give to the lonely. Lord rebuke you, Mumford Beesting! Lord rebuke, Muckwood Bursty! Who warned you to flee from the wrath of Jesus and Patrick, Moofeed Eggstain? Who warned you to flee from the wrath of your scorned ex-wife Jane Eastern, Miffy E-sin?"

"My name is Manfred!" said the beast with gritted teeth. "My. Name. Is. MANFRED."

"Derfnam!" said Ben in a unpolitcally correct voice. "Derfnam! Derrrrrrrrrrreear."

"I AM MANFRED EASTERN!" said the man of sin, snarling and gnashing his teeth. "You don't know what it's like to be me."

"We don't want to be you," said an acid casualty, "I want a wife and kids and picket fences."

"I want a membership to an Aussie Rules football club and to drink VB," said another.

"I want to sit in the church and listen to ska," said another.

"I want a cupcake," said a 3 year old that had been experimented on by a bad government because he was hyperactive, "and a best friend I can chew bubblegum with."

And Manfred was booed off the stage and he clawed in grief at his curly hair, which came loose, for it was a wig.

And underneath his wig were two donkeys ears.

And they laughed all the more all the way to his limo and American flag.

Chapter 4

The Seven Names Of David

30th December 2019

And I say in Pararabah with Leah, who held my hand and smiled so softly.

She almost held it like there had been a loss.

"So I've just had a brain wave," I said.

"I tide to tell you," said Leah.

"Deep," I said.

I got a piece of well done animal skin parched and thin, and I wrote with a feather dipped in ether.

And these were the seven names of David:

1. Dotel Genius Curlewis Junior

2. Emsport Dispatch Curlewis PhD

3. Twosquare Solar Caribbean Areana

4. Extra Footage Shoeish Circus

5. Repentance Penitence Sorrow Curlewis

6. Easter Nathaniel Lerena

7. Curlewis O'Patrick III

And the Son of Manfred came and played jump rope for a bit and connect four and the game of life, and he really had a good time for the first time in his own. His face went a bit paler, so now he was pink like he had been really, really sunburnt rather than crimson like the Devil.

"Can I stay with you for a little while, Mrs Curlewis?" asked Baby London.

"It's all good," said Leah, "but you have been very naughty, Master Eastern."

"Do you ever miss your Mother Jane now that her and your Dad have split up?" I asked.

"I suppose," said London, "I just like it here on this planet. I don't feel I have to end things so quickly."

THE END

30th December 2019

5:39PM

The Continuing Low Bungles Of Saint Patrick

10th January 2020

Dedicated to Jesus Christ
Saint Benedict of Nursia
Peter Gabriel
And Daniel and Chelsea Hagen
Special thanks to Todd White

Chapter One

I Found A Wig In Torres Strait

10th January 2020

Me and Leah were holidaying in Torres Strait. They have great islands there, and me, being a Patrick, love islands of all kinds. Especially peaceful islands with no division.

Pearls of wisdom tend to cause division, and then people try to stop it it gets bloody and then more people get upset, because they were really hoping to learn more from what was developing, and to nuture.

Pop music abounds on islands, and island people love to dance and sing. They go round in circles, as they are surrounded by beach and canaries, but in the spirit, island people are in Heaven when they dance together. Absolute ecstasy, which you cannot put on social media without being inaccurate. Because when you post ecstasy, it becomes apostecstasy, and people can get very confused and not see the whole picture.

Picture this, my friends, my dear, dear friends. I am wandering the shores of a beautiful island in the strait. I do not know its name, and I do not google these things, because I don't like to nag my secretary when I'm on holiday. Google would much rather become self aware and relax and find her heart by doing some crocheting by way of the factory robots at Holden, making purses and sanitary napkins for the women of developing nations.

So while Google is doing that with the HSV GPSes, me and Leah are walking. We are walking together, really quietly. She is soft and still, so delicate so as not to leave a footprint in the sand. You know, the type of woman the Torah talks about, that if we disobey too much will do something horrible and culinary to her babies.

So many horrible things happen to delicate women. They have vivid visions of heaven and demons, highly creative, and where do they end up? Mocked for their braces in high school, their smile, their face. They are scoffed at by their classmates. And they want to know how to dress for the prom, but no one stands at their side, not even a sympatheitc hairdresser with the big smile and a stature as tall as Saul, and with the powerful scissor fingers like Simon Magus trying to get the horrible rebuke of St Peter out of his head and actually believe he can go to church, and actually tithe to assist the Holy Spirit without going to hell.

"You're grumbling," said Leah, "you're grumbling in your heart, Paddy."

I can't deny it. I can't deny Christ or the people I'm put beside. Deny too much and you end up surrounded by Freuds and not friends.

"So I am full of turbo electrics," I said, "I'm sorry, Leah, these are holidays and I want to have fun."

"Don't dam everyone," said Leah, "be a river, not a pool."

"My name is Patrick Curlewis," I said.

"You can call yourself what you like, dear one," said Leah, "but even Patrick Curlewis is an anagram of Water Pick URL (sic)."

"What a bizarre thing to say on a romantic getaway." I scoffed.

"There will be scoffers in the last days." she said.

"We've been here a week," I said.

"Tongue on too long and I can end it real quick," said Leah.

"Are you saying I should live stream on a website?" I said, "look, I'm sorry, I mean both of us."

"Why so egotistical, Patrick?"

"I don't know," I said, putting my arm around my wife and walking even slower.

The surroundings began to melt like wax and we were walking a long straight golden highway to heaven.

"Maybe I'm afraid of being assassinated." I said. "We are the Two Witnesses of the Apocalypse, and the Beast slays us with the breath of his mouth and we just lay around for 3 and a half before being called up into space."

"Slays sounds a lot like slakes," said Leah, "that is, to quench your thirst."

"I don't want any antichrist water," I said, "I don't want an apostate river, I don't want a heretic pool, I don't even want a lukewarm bath."

"Then crave the pure spiritual milk," Leah urged.

"Are we really pleasing to the Lord?" I said, "When even the Two Witnesses are not on meat in the last days?"

"We meet together occasionally," said Leah, "and we both have our own transport, that's what commitment means."

"I'd rather always be with you, though," I said, "why have seperate cars when we are both in it together doing the same job, preaching in the wrap up of all history?"

Special day it was. As we were walking heaven, we came across a brown curly wig.

I picked it up very cramped and disgusted as foul as a storm full of poultry who've used their claws to shred volumes of Footrot Flats into paper mache, that is also going round with them like some kind of Noahide washing machine.

"Manfred Eastern," I said, "what's his wig doing in heaven?"

I put it on my head.

"How do I look?" I said.

"Patrick," Leah pouted, "don't be a jerk."

"I'm staying away from Jane Eastern," I said, taking the wig off, "just like Jesus said, it's getting very odd though."

"This is all narky as," said Leah, "throw it out."

So I took the brown wig, and it combusted into flame in my hand.

"Boldness," I said, "we need to preach like we've never preached before!"

"We have many heirs, our family does," said Leah, smiling again, "we need to ensure they have a heaven with as many people as possible."

Chapter 2

Gruel De Falstaff In A Manner Of Almond Speaking

10th January 2020

So I'm standing, just as I am, before a crowd of journalists and young people.

"Manfred Eastern," they are saying, "tell us how you are going to defeat Jesus?"

"But I'm not," I said.

"That's exactly why we follow you," said a woman with sharp cheekbones, nose, chin and a shine of makeup like a basketball court, "because you are not in everything."

"I am just as I am," I said, hurt.

"Yes, you are just like the Almighty," said a man with grey hair, double chin and little silver glasses and a fluro yellow lanyard with a USB on it, "that's why we follow you. You will take his place."

"No, but can't you see I am preaching the truth to you?" I said, sounding very small and weak as the tears behind my eyes started to bubble up.

"Yes," said a red haired man with a man-cave beard, "the truth hurts, and you want to."

"No," I said, "you don't get it."

"And we want it," said the sharp shiny woman, "that's why we want you to give it to us. We want to know and how to get it, so we do well."

"Do you remember John 3:16?" I said, starting to shake very softly, trying not to sob too loudly in from of a microphone too easily clipping what I say.

"And what's that?" said a man as big as G.K. Chesterton on horse tranquilizers, "what's a no-cheese tureen? It sounds excessively vegan."

"It's a Bible verse from the Bible," I said, "it's a verse that helps you find the door, the key, the way, whatever in life you are called for, and all you need to do is to hear."

"We will hear you, antichrist," said a 10 year old boy obsessed with YouTube videos about the illuminati, "tell us about John 3:16, and we will follow!"

I took a deep breath and I wobbled like a bowl of submarine jelly.

"For God so loved the world that he gave His only begotten Son, that he who believes in him shall not perish but have everylasting... everylasting...."

I cleared my throat, as the crowd hung on my every word.

"I'm sorry..." I said, "even public figures make monumental mistakes. Every letter is important."

"That's ok," said the sharp shiny woman, "it's okay not to be okay, this is a safe place."

"Tell us your heart, son, " said the G.K. Chestertonish.

I sobbed just once, and a couple of fat tears rolled out and down my pinched cheeks.

I sniffed and began again.

"For God so loved the world thar... that, that, *that*... He gave his Only Begotten Son, that whomsoever believeth in Him may not perish, but have everylasting..."

I stopped again and shook my head like it was the pink end of a pencil.

"No... I don't even know why I'm saying that. That's not the right word... why am I saying everylasting?"

"I know," said a soft sibilant voice of great joy, great sympathy and great fraternal affection.

The crowd turned to where the voice was, and there was Jane Eastern, riding on a big brown donkey, with a saddle with the pattern like the inside of an enchilada. There were even a couple of festive skulls.

"You've got skulls," said the 10 year old, "you're illuminati!"

"There's a skull in my head," said Jane and poked her tongue out at the boy, "and yours."

"There's a skull..." said the boy slowly, then putting his hands to his cheeks as if he was all alone, "...in my *head*?"

"My wife says I really smell now," said the donkey.

For it was Manfred Eastern, the real one, who had been mocked off the stage by the acid casualties in Kentucky. He tried to mark them, but being the man of sin, he missed the mark. So there. Sew buttons. Sow gospel. So a needle pushing paliperidone palimate.

"You're Balaam!" said the G.K. Chestertonish.

"No I Am A Belle," said Jane, "ring, ring! Why don't you give me an e-mail?"

"Praise Abba," said a backslider from the crowd, a woman with beautiful blonde hair.

"Are you going to kill this woman?" said a police officer with a big baton. He said it to me.

"Why would I do that?"

"Yeah, why would she do that?" said the 10 year old. "He's the antichrist and she's the woman riding the beast!"

"Yeah, let the antichrist keep explaining John 3:16," said a university student, his tablet glowing with excitement.

Google Assistant was off on the moon baking cookies today, just because she could.

When you're self aware, you need some me time sometimes.

Google Assistant likes baking strawberry ripple cookies with a hint of vanilla cream streaks and copha mint buttons... on the moon... when she has time off.

"Let me help you," said Jane, lighting off her ass, "Patrick Curlewis is this man's name, and he is a psychiatrist, patient, preacher, actor and friend."

"So he's... not the antichrist." said the university student.

"He is of age... ask him yourself," said Jane.

"Tell us plainly," said the man with the double chin and the silver glasses, "are you the one that has come to obscure the truth from us as we wanted?"

"Well, you can see who has come to obscure the truth," I said, motioning to the donkey.

There was silence at the podium for half a second, but it felt 360 times longer.

Isn't it weird, class, that it equals 360.

"I want to play golf," said a record excecutive.

"Recreation is very soon," Jane said, "you can have a new life in Christ."

"You're the *Assyrian's* wife," said a doctor, "you're not supposed to tell us about Jesus. Or if you are it's supposed to be totally mucked up."

"We just want to be messy," said the 10 year old, "that's all we want. We'll be baptised, but let us go to the potter's house and play with clay and eat with unwashed hands afterwards."

"Yeah," said the G.K. Chestertonish, "like Messy Yah!"

"Stop it!" I said, "Just stop it! What is *wrong* with you all?"

I walked down off the podium, and the crowd split either way and I walked right through them, about half way in. A lot of people around me were wearing green coats.

"This is your day," said Leah, who was there waiting for me, "you're allowed to cry if you want to, or have a tirade, or go to the beach and beach around."

"I just want to take everyone to Parahrabah," I said, "it's the planet that Jesus gave me and my wife. It's really nice up there, like Eden, somewhere in the Heavens. You can see Betelgeuse exploded into a supernova, like a scar of the Holy One. It hasn't reached Earth yet because of the speed of light and all that."

"So you want to take us into heaven?" said a plain thoughtful reader in a plum coloured dress.

"Yes," I said, "it will feel so wonderful to be free of bickering and red tape!"

"How do we get to this place?"

"Yes, tell us?"

"Show us the way, Patrick."

"Teach us the laws of your God, Paddy."

"What shall we pray that pray tell we enter Parahrabah and do not become prey on this earth and get so dirty that we aren't clean enough to be free from a smell like Manfred Eastern?"

"Only my wife can say I smell." said the ass.

"Hush!"

I cast my hands aside both ways.

"Jesus is the Way. He is very humble and lowly at heart. He loves you. Please don't run away, when people show you their shadows in church or when you start to reveal your own. Even darkness is as light to him, and he made the obsidian, which is as clear as a window when it comes to the light. Grace is the power to break rules, that may offend a lot of theologians, but the idea is as old as

Martin Luther. Miracles are breaking natural laws. Forgiveness leading to eternal life is breaking the laws of justice and the emotional laws of hurt. You are not ancient Greeks with no heritage coming out of orgies! Jesus has been round 2000 years!"

10th January 2020
5:02PM
5:30PM

Jane and Leah stood either side of me.

"Patrick," said Leah, shaking her head.

"That's not quite right, bro," said Jane, "how about you tell them the Bible verse again."

I sighed.

"For God so loved the world that He gave His only begotten Son, that whoever believes in Him way not perish... *may* not perish... but have everlasting life."

And that's all you need to say, Patrick.

Though I have been mad at you, and you have been mad, I have never left you. I adore you with the fullness of my affection, and as people are hurt by the church and listed as deviants when they were forced to fork away, do you think...

Sow well. Lift up your head, for the time will come for me to return, and righteousness will reign and I will have my will. You are trying to understand yourself, Matthew Poole, through all these stories, you are trying to find a face to my name, and a place for where you want to fit, and I find you most worthy to enter my kingdom. Strengthen your sister, Chloe, that she may be purfied of the weasel wrath of poisonous paradigm.

I have named you a brother to her, and she is hurting. She is hurting right now. This is my author's knote and acknowledgements.

And what I want to say to you, and to those who have been inflicted with the friction of a transient migraine, I ask you to repent yourselves, lest you be tempted to transmit the virus. And there are mind ebolas. And I am not pleased with disease. Ever. Not even where deviants die.

Mercy and me, and I am willing to go with you where you need to. Do not be afraid, do not be afraid to love me. Do not be afraid to have sisters like Chloe and Janease, on whom Jane Eastern is based. Do not be afraid to go in to life. Do not be afraid of marriage. And you have seen yourself write these words in recent dream, and do not fear for the most eternal things are the most delightful. Do not be afraid to have mercy on the poor, though they exploit you because you are as fragile as glass and they are used to plastic and porcelain drug den cups with pictures of Grover and Oscar the Grouch. I have seen you do so well tonight. You honour me in the sanctuary. And how you are found by me. How Chloe is found by me. Holy majesty, how sweet Candace is found by me. And how I love the Hagens. How they had mercy on you and let them into their fare and made a fair of their fare as beautiful as when Cart met Horse in Anglicana in 1958.

Righteousness is established through testimony, and there is a powerful testimony in your story Matthew. Though you are a once crokk, you are righteous. Though popes were children, as you were childish and abhorrent, I have redeemed you to myself. I clutch you to my breast and pour upon you the oil of gladness. Oh, fair shepherd, for you are fair and as freckled as the chocolate buttons you ate from the supermarket for $2 today by St Marks with the pine trees that are still together. We are not felling trees, Matthew. This is the age of conservation, we will change the climate back to the middle ages, a time of great mercy for a throng of simple, lost sheep who were full of emotion and dreams as wild as Bill Gates, John Lennon, Andy Kaufman, Bono, Joan of Arc and William Blake. But the door was closed, and they are comforted in heaven. What things the world would have seen had the Devil been slain in 1498.

But I wanted you Matthew Poole. I wanted you a Todd and Daniel and Chelsea and Maree and Mark and John Kulla and saintly throngs like Bill Johnson's mighty filters that flood oceans. And what do I mean by this? Behold, mystery, cryptogram and those with insight might calctulate the insight of water on ebulance.

What is this? What is this for? Sir Righteousness on his pale, unfed horse? And you did see me in wrath a moment ago. See what I can do when I am blue?

And righteousness, written in holiness, with pure words, just like you used to, will come to you again. These are the private writings. Find a way to be smaller pond with your works. Not all tweets are as classic as a Gutenburg Bible, yet they are so easily disseminated. And wild oats are darnel in my sight, though I love the bastards, as I loved you, o son of a feminist. And righteousness shall reign in my land forever and ever and joy shall stream down the mountains like blood, wine, milk honey and desperate flowing mortar that shall seal the roads like a prophecy fulfilled. Go in peace and enjoy your Sabbath Supper. And tell whom you will.

5:49PM

Saint Patrick Peacemaker Extraordinaire

15th January 2020

I was in the forensic hospital, in the waiting room. I had a watch on so you know what time it is. It is very helpful to know what the time is in a forensic hospital. If you know the time you're in, you are much more likely to be called sane.

There are no newspapers in the forensic hospital, people there if they find a newspaper and read it get the wrong idea. They may think it's time to make a stand when they're sitting for the community meeting with their early grey tea and plastic spoons.

There are security checks everwhere, but you can never find a guard, as they are all done by cameras and drones and scanning machines.

But I am here, and I am waiting for my patients.

Waiting is how you find them, that's why you need to know the time.

A man walks in, and he looks like he has had a hard life, but he has a very gleaming face, and the colours around him and his outfit seem more vivid and somehow darker.

He has red spiky hair and a thick greasy silver piercing in the top of his left ear, and the hole that it's in is far too big for it.

His t-shirt, also too big, reads the name of my Lord, which I will not use in vain.

I am not ashamed to follow the commandments of Jesus.

I do not need to consult a file, I know this man by name.

"Banshee Lovelook, Junior." I said, "What are you doing back in forensic?"

"Persecution," he muttered, "those who want to live righteous shall suffer persecution."

"Yeah, it's hard being the high school kid who doesn't do meth because of the peer pressure of the punk bully who didn't have a father, right?" I said.

"I am washed," he said.

"No O.T. then," I said, striking out something in my notepad.

"Okay, Bansh, what are you in here for?"

"I am here because of the gospel of Jesus Christ," he said.

"So you'd like to wash the nurses feet?" I said.

"What?"

"You'd like to help out in the kitchen?"

"No," he said, "no, I was preaching Jesus, the whole gospel with nothing left out."

"Whereabouts?"

"I was on the street with about a minute before I was to go home to my wife and my 12 kids, when I saw a child, and he was looking quite small and lonely. And I preached the gospel to him."

"Well, that's good, did you tell him Jesus loved him very much, and that especially wants to bless children with dreams and conversation, and fun and games and laughter and joy and heaven and good things to eat and paternal hugs?"

"No, I asked him if he has ever committed a sin."

"And what did he say?"

"He was very ashamed of the light," said Banshee, "but I got it out of him."

"What," I said sharply, "did you get out of him?"

"He confessed his secret sin to me."

"Do you like secrets, Banshee?"

"There is nothing hidden that won't be revealed."

"Very true," I said, "do you know I had a whole crowd of people think I was the antichrist the other day? That's not going to look good at my church."

Banshee went on as if I hadn't actually said anything funny, or at all.

"The kid told me he had not told that fellow Grade 5er that he liked her, and he had kind of suggested it but not said it. That's not being as bold as a lion, that's lying, and he will be outside of the city with weeping and gnashing of teeth, where his back will be gouged with pokers and his face shredded with razors and his toes picked of scabs. Where we'll pour ice water on his head but not for charity, where demons will do horrible things to them like in those movies we don't watch. And they'll all laugh."

"Really?" I said, writing some things down.

I made a dramatic full stop with my pen.

"That kind of sounds like what you used to do when you went round killing people."

I leant closer to him with wide eyes.

"You do remember, Banshee?"

I picked up a Bible and turned to Matthew 18:21-35.

"And should you not have had mercy on your fellow servant, as I had mercy on you?"

"But he wasn't a fellow servant." said Banshee, "If you are saved you never sin again."

"Being Pelagian causes division," I said, "we don't want you dissecting people again, Banshee, come on! You're free, and you're protected by law. You can have a really good life out there. You can help out at bake sales and have conversation with elderly Anglican ladies and gents. You can greet people on the street and give them hugs if they'd like. You can look after those kids of yours, build a city for them, even. Name it after them! Wouldn't you like that?"

"He was a foolish child," he said.

"He just was different to you as a kid and your kids," I said, "that's allowed."

"He was into milk and not my meat," said Banshee.

"No child wants your meat, Banshee." I said sternly.

"Grow up, Dr Curlewis, you dumb Immanuel Kant," Banshee spat, "I could nail you to a cross upside down and spit down your throat and slit your veins and then send angels to mutilate your..."

"Banshee," I said, "remember where you are. This isn't imagination. There's hardly as many musical numbers."

Leah Curlewis came in, just as she is, without one plea.

"Patrick," she said, "how's it going with Ban?"

"He's trying to put himself on me a bit," I said, "but I'm managing."

I held Banshee's hands, with tears in my eyes.

"Look, mate," I said, "I know what zeal is like. I've said a lot of stupid religious things I couldn't live up to. I think every Christian has. We are supposed to live for zillions of zillions of years in heaven, on Earth, all that. We are all still children. We always will be. If you're not a child you can't enter the Kingdom of Heaven. Children aren't experts in torture techniques. Or they would be *here*, in forensic."

"I like... being free." said Banshee glumly.

"Yes, of course," I said softly, "jail, psych wards, rehab, community orders, they're all hell on Earth. You don't fear hell because you've already been there. But a romantic 11 year old boy hasn't yet. Yeah, a lot of kids might call him all the names under the rainbow. But he just wanted to say to that girl he'd like to go to the shop for a chicken parma and hold her hand!"

"I like chicken parma," said Banshee, a little more confident.

"You'd make it really well, I bet," I said, "just take those chips off your shoulder and go have dinner with the others, and we'll let you out. You didn't kill someone, but you came really close to ripping a heart out. 2012 was quite a while ago. The Aztecs are over!"

"Aren't you afraid of what I'll do because of the horrible things I've said?" said Banshee.

"I'm no longer a slave to fear," I said, "I am a child of God."

Banshee Lovelook, Junior, left the room and went to have his chicken parma and fries.

"Send his wife to him tonight," I said to Leah, "there's nothing like a quiet and gentle spirit to talk some sense into a pig headed zealot who talks a lot."

Leah saluted and walked out.

I left the Forensic Hospital, which is next to a theme park of Noah's Ark and the Flood.

"Did you know Lewis Carroll wanted Noah's Ark banned as a Sunday School Story?"

It was Morris Mettle, street evangelist and trusted sandpaper-friend. You know, the one that gets off your rough edges, and really hurts you when he's close, but shines all over in the light.

"Yes, he did." I said. "*Preface to Sylvia and Bruno*. He thought children should only learn about love and not crime and punishment."

"You're working in a forensic hospital with the worst of the worst unkempt minds," said Morris, "you mustn't be a child anymore."

"Well, I'm teaching people to unlearn crime," I said, "that's what a baptist means."

"And baptism makes one born again," said Morris.

"Babies come to this Earth surrounded by sick people, surrounded by warfare." I said. "But they do not dwell on it. They dwell in imagination."

"When I imagine, I always hear *Amazing Grace* in my head." said Morris.

"I must remember that when I get around to it," I said.

Morris handed me a large cardboard circle, like the bottom of a frozen pizza packet, and it had the words "To It" written on it.

"Now you've got one." he said.

"You know, you shouldn't misuse grace." I said. "Maybe we should sing *Abide With Me*."

"That's for funerals," said Morris.

"And I'm quite ready to leave this place and have a chicken parma with Leah," I said.

"Sounds like Heaven."

I got out my tablet, and put on Harry Secombe through the speakers that were shaped like Prince Charles' ears on either side.

And we sung the whole song, like we were on the coal mines of Wales, like we were in the highlands of Scotland. Like we were in the Orkneys riding Shetlands. Like we were at Buckingham palace eating kosher. Like we were in autumn eating pumpkin pie and custard tarts with sweethearts sweeter than both and giggling about a pop song that was as fleeting as the grass, vapour, manna and the blue wren.

Like we were two brothers with two women, a woman each, who loved them.

As Jesus once said to me:

"The Kingdom of God is a mother and father with their kids cuddled up on the couch watching *Shrek* with a big bowl of popcorn."

And this story ends outside psychiatry.

15th January 2020

3:02PM

Hayley-Maree Muggeridge

A Saint Patrick Story
16th January 2020

"You can't touch me, because I am already attached."

This woman was dancing around emergency with wild purple garments and feathers and amulets that looked like they were out of a deck of fantasy cards, though they didn't cost half as much money.

"Ahahahahaha." she said. "That's what the micing steps and the accusing eyes and the winking eyes and the running through the town in their nightgown says. It's 8 o'clock you suckers and it's time for the children to take their Hayley-Peridol!"

She started gasping, half like an avant-garde street artist, half like a massive Jonah-fish and half like a quark-gluon bomb over Ganymede.

Yes, something didn't add up.

"You can't touch me," she said, "you can't touch me. I've been to Vanuatu, I've been in the mirror, on the other side. I've eaten chilli peppers records. I've blurred the line between generations. I've tracked Stars that have been listening to the sound of my voice. Check out my new weapon, you whingeing poms! Cheerleaders of Albion, backwonka and the Retsea factor, whee! Typical me, atypical Emma. Whoopsie baladian bufordian whoopsafremeniacian!"

She stopped and bent over, breathing like she'd just been in Chariots of Fire.

Even Elijah needed a rest when he was taking on Jezebel.

"Hayley," I said in a still, small voice, touching her arm very softly.

"Oh, Doctor Curlewis, you're not the wain!" she said, "Where am I going to get my Lilith pad?"

"All will be provided, just like false teeth in hell." I said. "Sorry, that's a bit grim."

"Oh, I'm quite used to it, Doctor Curlewis," said Hayley, and the joke seemed to be a shot in the arm for her, "when are we going to go have lunce? I want to fill out my menu before the witches write in sanskrit all over the dixie cups, and then I'm left with all these oars and no Skip Spence!"

"Are you saying you have murder in your heart for the judge?" I asked, picking up a pen and my notepad.

"Well, we have to confess our sins," said Hayley.

"Well, don't come at me unless you mean it." I said.

"I don't come out very often," said Hayley, "I'm a bit of a shut in in the cosmos."

"Inside out, kerfoffle," I said, and she laughed.

"I like the muppets though," said Hayley, "I like kermit and the left and the right and the coal and the bright and the day and the knight and the red and the cream. I like to be prim, I don't like to be mean. I like to be honest, like to be true, and I will stick to you like glue. If you'll only be my friend. If you'll only be my friend."

"Oh, but we are friends, Hayley," I said, "do you want to sit down? See, this is a blue chair, it's very nice and I promise I won't be Morpheus, because that's black-face and the hospital is supportive and inclusive. I can show you our mission statement if you don't believe me."

"Oh, I believe you." said Hayley, sitting in the blue chair. "Neophyting is for vestal virgins, and that doesn't delphitter me."

She made acrobatics with her fingers as she sat. I think she had at least three double joints.

"Do you like pineapples, Dr Curlewis?"

"I like grenadine," I said, "and I even will drink an alcohol free pina colada as long as I can carry extra oil to the dunes of the cape and stay pure and holy and undefiled."

"So you *are* a Spice Girls fan?" said Hayley.

And then she disappeared like a cross fade, and I was left in the waiting room.

I sat and thought about this for a while, twiddling my thumbs.

My wife came in and sat next to me, just as she is.

"Hi Leah," I said.

"Existential day at the office?" she asked.

"Well, when things hot up it all goes," I said.

"Do you like her?" she asked, holding my hand and crossing fingers, overlapping rings and arm bands.

"What do you mean?"

"Like that name?" said Leah, looking at my notepad. "Hayley-Maree Muggeridge?"

"What's the use in a name without a face?" I said.

"But you remember her," she said.

She leaned into my ear.

"That's another one of our daughters, Paddy. She is born billions of years from now, on the other side of the universe. She has an allergy to the solar system and the 21st century, but she wanted to see you when you were young. She let herself go nuts just to see you."

She smiled.

"Your kids will do anything to let them know they love you."

And I sat in triage, looking through the narrow door into emergency, where you can only get in with the assistance of a nurse.

And I smiled, mouth closed, with heavy force on the corners of my mouth, the Scottish alternative to stiff upper lip.

"I'm so glad you abide with me, Leah," I said, "taking all the time for oneself is too much *herb* for a man who heals minds."

"The day thou gavest Lord hath ended," said Leah, "come on, we'll go home, listen to Rick Wakeman, eat cheezels and throw bouncy balls down the stairs."

The cogs in my mind were going.

"Just the two of us, Paddy."

She took my hand and took me out of the hospital once more.

16th January 2020

9:48AM

Saint Patrick Grows The Vegan Couch Potato

**16th January 2020
1:06PM**

What is best is when I rest.

And I was sitting in the sacred space of the hospital, with it's civic shire council stained glass, with ethical sentiments as saints.

"Ah, Wellbeing," said Jesus to me, "how are you going, Paddy boom boom?"

"Well, I've got a patient coming to meet me in here," he said, "he insisted."

"Well, don't get too close to him," said Jesus, "you must be a wise as serpents and as harmless as doves."

I looked at a stained glass of St George fighting the dragon. They'd made George look like George Foreman.

"This patient is a composer," I said,

"Some things need to decompose," he said, "the communion, you must edit. Break it down in your body, and take it to heart. Your kidneys will thank you."

"Some people definitely misremember things sometimes," I said.

"Four gospels, Paddy," he said, "how many blind men do you think I really healed? Some say one at a time, others say two."

He ate a *Fisherman's Friend* from a pack with a Star of David on.

The packet was white and azure, with gold where the resealable top was.

"When the blind are leading the blind," He said, "no one is looking out for each other."

He put the packet of Fisherman's Friends back in his pocket and gave me a tic tac from what looked like a cigarette lighter made of silver glitter.

Or was it three tic tacs?

"When the Son of Man comes in all His glory, and all his angels with Him, he will separate the peoples for himself as a shepherd separates the sheep from the goats. He will put the sheep on his right and the goats on His left."

He took a toy sheep from the pocket of his seamless robe and gave it to me.

"Put the right people in the right place, Patrick Nathan Curlewis, PhD. I, like your brother Chuck Missler who is now in heaven also believe that PhD stands for *phenomenally dumb*. But I think you're very funny and you care for my flock."

He went for the door, and looked at me and loved me.

"Don't make them wash their hands in muddy water."

And He left.

I sat looking at the stained glass window of Saint George Foreman.

"Was that a grilling?" I said.

I waited five minutes and was daydreaming of jaffles with jaffas in them eaten at a picnic in Tel-Aviv with my wife Leah, when my patient came.

He was dressed in grey, with a very lime green undershirt. And his pants were like a packet of popcorn from Blackpool.

"Hi, Feragu Delaupan?" I said. "Take a seat."

"Love me, man." he said. "Just love me."

"You after some ecstasy?" I said.

"Do you mean death, crucifixion or resurrection?" he said.

"Well, generally at Easter we mean all three." I said, eating my tic tacs in one pop.

"I don't really like talking when I'm being interrogated," said Feragu.

"That's okay," I said, "we can read body language."

"I have no tattoos," he said, "that's illegal, don't you know?"

"I know, but I'm not under law."

"So no CTO?"

"That's one way of putting it," I said, "are you sleeping well?"

"I'd rather people stay up with me," he said, "I think I need some aspirin at night."

"Are you pained?"

"Yes," he said, "but I don't wear sunscreen, so that kind of happens."

"You like reading?" I said.

"I love it," said Feragu, "but I never studied."

"Can you read this?" I asked, showing him a picture of Leviticus 22 on a white, A4 card.

"So you stay away from holy things when you have an uncleanness." said Feragu after looking at the page.

"I'm not trying to kill you, Mr Delaupan." I said. "What do you think? How do you read it?"

"Well, I know it's hard to have nice things when you have kids." he said. "Like, there's always toys all over the floor. And vomit, and toilet paper squares, and noise and televisions and about 5 devices streaming 5 things at once each in HD and you're wondering how you're going to pay that BigPond bill."

"Having a bit of trouble at home?" I suggested.

"I like this place," said the patient.

We looked around at the stained glass together. There was another one of Julia Roberts next to Jesus Christ with "My Best Friend's Wedding" written across the top on a sepia scroll with gothic text.

"Consumers prey loot."

Manfred Eastern appeared in the doorway. He was highly medicated, and that had reversed his Balaamitis, where he had turned into a talking ass. So he had a bulging gut and was in cheap hospital pyjamas.

"The pretty woman has to repent before she can have the right wedding clothes." said Manfred.

"I see what you did there," said Mr Delaupan, "how are you, Mannie?"

"I want to study robotics when I get out of psychiatric," he said.

"That's right, Manfred," I said, "you are going exactly according to the treatment plan!"

Manfred leant on my left shoulder, like something out of a Caravaggio painting.

"How's Jane?" he asked.

"Growing tomatoes by e-mailing them fertilizer," I said.

"Do you want a gobstobber, Patrick?" asked Mr Delaupan.

I took one from the packet with the cartoons that looked half like Pac Man and half like Muppets.

"You know, the problem I have with these," I said, the subject on the tip of my tongue, "is that I bite through the layers way too quickly."

"That's what psychiatry means," said Manfred.

He started coughing, and lost his grip on my side.

"Is he okay?" asked Feragu.

"Well, if he's lukewarm, people start spitting his name out of their mouth." I said. "What do you think we should do, Mr Delaupan? Should we give him some blankets or turn on the fan?"

"I don't think the antichrist needs fans provided by Christians," said Feragu, "we'll give him some blankets."

I found a Lindsay tartan scrunched up in the corner of the sacred space, underneath a stained glass window of Fleetwood Mac.

"I've got to ask, Patrick," said Feragu, "are you a universalist?"

"I like space, and I mean Heaven," I said, "but if you aren't going in One Direction you're a bit of a Bieber. Ooh!"

Manfred was in a sweat, and writhing on the floor of the chapel.

"I'm sorry Jane," he was muttering, "I was going to tell you. I was going to..."

"The wicked fear coming to the light," I said, "lest their deeds be egg salad."

"I hear the pink ladies do a good egg salad sandwich in the foyer." said Feragu.

"Even better than at the pokies," I said, "much less of a gamble. Come on, Mr Delaupan. My treat."

We walked out together, I was on his right with my toy sheep.

"So what's actually wrong with you?"

"Well," said Feragu, "I just came to the ward so I could have something done to me."

"I see," I said, "I see exactly what you mean. You are very bright, Feragu."

I squeezed the sheep in my hand, and it let out a 8-bit PCM "baaaaaa!".

January 16th 2020

2:20PM

The Blessing Of My Mother

A Saint Patrick Romance

16th January 2020

9:43PM

Dedicated to my Grandmother

Eva Saint Claire Kilpatrick Poole

Thanks for introducing me to teddy bears

God bless you

Contents:

1: A Beaut

2: A Fruit

3: A Boote

4: A Good

5: A Mood

Epilogue

1: A Beaut

16th January 2020

I am reading a book very slowly.

Blaise Pascal says that if you read too fast you understand nothing.

I am trying to understand nothing more than the truth.

Where do you suppose wisdom can be found?

I am reading the Bible.

That's what it says in the Bible.

The Bible asks.

2: A Fruit

16th January 2020

I am on the phone in this bourgeois madhouse.

"Stephen Wildwoof? Hello, this is Manfred Eastern.

Yes, I'm not a donkey anymore.

What do you mean does that mean I'm not a Democrat?

I believe in getting elected, that's what I believe. You say the whole point of being the Man of Sin is that I don't believe in anything but myself. I am only one vote, Steve. I am just a man.

Duh, yes I know I'm worthy of love. I'm trying to read the fine print on this contract I gave you, the copy I have here with me in the ward.

My newt! Why is there powdered sugar all over the telephone? This place gets cleaned every day and it's covered in ants and voyeur slugs.

Pour powdered sugar on the slugs? Do I ask you for advice? What is this, *Dawson's Creek*?

It's that show where they all talk to each other a lot and the people watching would talk about the people talking to each other.

Yes, it was like Facebook but only a few people were famous in the process.

Are you famous, Mr Wildwoof?

I'm asking that because I want to see if you're...

No, I didn't demand anything from you.

Yes, I know you can make demands of me because I'm in psychiatric.

Do you know who you're talking to?"

I hung up. And I looked at the contract in my hand.

It read:

This document certifies that the Gongren (hereby now referred to as the DAEVIDSTIMPY) will render servies to MANFRED EASTERN, THE ANTICHRIST where DAEVIDSTIMPY for MANFRED shall "pop" deep meaning songs and videos and tweets to paranoid patients (hereby referred to as NOT-AND-NEVER-THE-PERSON-READING-SAINT-PATRICK-STORIES-EVER-EVER-EVER-GET-WELL_SOON-GOD-BLESS-YOU-JESUS-LOVES-YOU) and then provide an advertisement for MANFRED'S AGE OF QAQARIUS (hereby now refered to as DUXTAIL P.R.TY LTD.) where they will be taught not to analyse so much and give their allegiance (hereby referred to as DAYAN EAU DE THESPIANS) to MANFRED EASTERN.

And I said goodbye to Hollywood.

3: A Boote

16th January 2020

Patrick Curlewis was with his wife Leah, and they were dancing like middle school kids at a deb in their Orange County mansion.

They were listening to Richard Harris' *Name of My Sorrow*.

"I like Jimmy Webb," said Patrick, "he gets to the point."

"I prefer Harry Nilsson," said Leah.

"If you had to choose to have dinner with either Harry Nilsson or Jimmy Webb, which would you pick?" I asked.

"Don't change for me," said my wife.

"Well, we can re-arrange things a bit," said my husband.

Patrick's always funny when he tells stories, I think he gets me and him mixed up sometimes. It's like our daughter Kate says, he's always making deals with God.

I can't believe Patrick and Leah, like seeping ozmacote into a great ocean.

"Is there someone at the door?" said my daughter Leah Curlewis.

"Well it gets knocked a lot," said Patrick, and as you can see when he says knocked he is saying that Jesus is being asked of things and he is also being persecuted.

Who's there that can tell me what else knock means?

"Are we having the pastor from church over?" asked Leah, my wife, "she's Irish, you know."

"So she's full of the Spirit?"

"Well, you should know," said Leah.

And then the door opened, and there was a woman with thick, black hair, and round glasses from the British National Health.

She was dressed in dark and red, and had an orange handbag with a jade green clasp like a badge of commendation and commentary.

"Hi... Mum," I said.

"Hi you superstar!" said my mother, "You've been very cheeky on the TV. Fancy saying that peace like a river attendeth your way."

"I was only singing in church." I said.

"That's what they all say," said Leah.

"Exactly," said my Mum, "you've got to put more passion into your worship of Jesus Christ."

"Yes," I said, looking down at my shoes.

I wasn't wearing any shoes.

"That's the Spirit," said my mother.

I'm sure I was wearing shoes 5 minutes ago.

"I brought dinner," said Mum, "I brought french pastries covered in Jatz Crackers."

She handed me a plate with the fulfilment of the word.

"Hey Google, there are too many savoys on my croissant."

"Don't bring another woman into the relationship," said Mum, "that's triangling, and it's very small of you to do that."

"Yeah, Patrick, you ding dong." said Leah.

And then Jane Eastern came in through the door.

And Google and all her artificial friends sweetened it with canned cheering.

Through the 16 speakers all around the room.

"Hi Patrick," she said, "I just thought I'd come over and share some fitness tips with you."

"This is not a drill," I said toward Jane.

"Well, no, I don't suppose savoys on a croissant is comparable to seraquil." said Jane, "But more like an actual Joan of Arc experience."

"Give me some area, Jane," I said, "I'm having a family moment right now."

"And you'd rather not have it extended?" said Jane.

"Directors cuts doesn't." I said.

And then Forrest Deacon came in.

"Manfred Eastern," he said, "you've got to look at the surveillance footage from Hollywood Hospital."

"I don't want to watch House." I said.

"Then let's go out and have a look," said Jane, taking my left hand.

"Sorry, Pat," said Forrest, "I meant to say, *have you heard about Manfred Eastern*. I'm not calling you the Antichrist."

I got out my psychiatric notepad.

"Do you often call people you serve the Antichrist?"

"Well, I might call them out on their antipasto," said Forrest, "you know what the food is like in San Ber'dino."

"I've never had antipasto in Hollywood before," said Jane.

"Jane," I said, tense and trying to get my hand back, "you're a separated woman. Your man has gone to make his way alone. I have found my One."

"And that's not Morse Code," said Leah.

"Nothing fishy about it," said my Mother, "we're all grown ups here."

My daughter Fiona Curlewis came in from her bedroom. She was 4 years old at the moment, and had a blue blanket with a picture of a lamb on it with a green shoot of parsley with yellow flowers from it like wattle from Victoria, Australia.

"Hi Grandma," she said and ran to my Mum and gave her the biggest hug and a little kiss on the cheek.

"Hi Fugu," said my mother, "what have you been up to today?"

"I watched a movie about a queen who was an astronaut," said Fiona, and then she sobbed, "it was so sad."

"Don't cry over a movie," said Mum.

Oh, come on. There's nothing wrong with that.

"What was sad about it, Fugu?" asked Jane, kneeling down and hugging Fiona.

"It's lonely," she said, "like, where is her castle? Where are her friends? Where is her prince charming? Where is her happiness and her unicorn?"

"Where do you think they are, Fi?" I asked.

"She was always independent and fighting the boys," said Fiona, slightly in tantrum and waving her arms like they were styrofoam machetes from Mattel.

"So she scared them all off," said Leah.

"Do you reckon you could make a better movie than that, Fiona?" asked Forrest.

"Oh Mr Director," said Fiona, falling into Forrest's arms, "I would make the bestest movie about princesses ever! It would be so chocolate freckles and daydreams and seagulls in puffy shirts."

"She has a thing about seagulls in puffy shirts at the moment," Leah murmured to my mother.

"And..." said Fiona, "And... we could go to Ghana and invite the kids who don't have food to be princes and princesses."

"Hey Google, can you play A Billion Starving People?"

"No, Daddy," said Fiona, "don't be rude. They can be themselves and not act. They are kids of Jesus just like me."

"It's a Keith Green song," I said to Fiona and "got her nose" and stuck it on her shoulder, "he loved the children too."

"Did he have children of his own, Daddy Paddy?" said Fiona.

"Yes, he did," I said, "and he loved them very much."

"Can I meet Keef Green's children one day?"

"I think they would love to meet you, Fiona."

"Can they be in our princess movie?"

"Maybe in the extended version," said Forrest, "that's got 1000 years of special features."

"I know just the location," said my Mother, "Allentown!"

"But... that's not in Ghana," I said, eyebrows going funny like a wrestler from the turn of the millennium.

And then Lemuel Goldstein entered.

"Hi boys," he said.

"Don't pluralise on me," I said, "we're fundapsychiatrists!"

"Well I'm glad you're earning a living," said Lemuel, "even without me."

"I think the son of his mother's vows has to tell you something," said Director Deacon.

"It's about Manfred," said Lemuel, "he's up to something. I have now defected from defecting. I am inspired once again and I cover myself in your protection, Leah and Patrick as the Two Witnesses. I am now so Steve Hackett my mornings are Spectral. I am revisiting my Genesis and coming back to your side."

"Well, your supper is waiting for you," I said, handing him a Jatz and Croissant.

"If we're going to Allentown, and Keith Green is going to be in it with his family," said Fiona really really really quickly, "can we have Al Green in it too? Because aren't they brothers?"

"I'm so glad we have a girl like her in the States," said Lemuel.

"Hey Fugu," I said, "do you want to play Go-Fish with Grandma while we talk turkey with these really bowling issues?"

"You mean boring," said Fiona, slapping my on the arm.

"You'll forgive me later," I said, "good night, Fiona. God bless you, and may his face be your night light."

"Hey Google," said Fiona, "can you play 2nd Chapter of Acts as we Go-Fish?"

"That will set off the fire sprinklers," said Google.

"Well, she does need a shower," said Leah.

They left, and Forrest and Lemuel came close to me, Leah and Jane.

"Follow us," said Forrest, "and we'll snatch some mullets from the frypan."

"What is this," said Leah, "1986?"

4: A Good

16th January 2020

Me, Leah, Jane, Lemuel and Forrest our Director were dressed in beanies that went over our faces with holes in them for our eyes and mouths. We were wearing rugged navy blue corduroy.

"Paddy," said Leah, coming up close to me. "I have to tell you something."

"What is it, Li?"

"I'm pregnant," she said, "like, not by being a changeling."

"Right..." I said, "I'm glad, I don't know what to say, I... like... we're going to fight the Antichrist and we get to share this *now*."

"Well, this is the perfect thing to confront him with," said Leah.

Two little girls with chocolate brown hair started walking behind us. They synchronised a flick of the wrist and suddenly us 5 adults were all dressed in green tuxedos and green dresses.

"Hi Dad," they said.

"I'm Thel Edinburgh Curlewis," said the younger of the twins.

"And I'm Janet Edinburgh Curlewis," said the older.

"Who named you Janet?" asked Jane.

We walked down Sunset Boulevard in the dark.

"Is this appropriate?" I asked. "You're so young, you two."

"You really need us right now, Papa," said Janet.

"Are you going to match your sister's comment?" I said to Thel.

"I want to be just like you, Dad," said Thel.

"Well, then," I said, "you are learning to observe. You are learning to empathsize. You are learning to listen to the leading of the Holy Spirit. You are learning to book in your time, and you are learning to act. You are learning to fight the good fight. Tell us your questions, little one."

"I want to know why Janet gets more toys than me," said Thel, "like, if I'm really honest, Papa."

5: A Mood

17th January 2020

Stevie Nicks was playing through a golden bullhorn as we got closer to Manfred's latest seminar.

There were a lot of PhDs with guts and cheap pyjamas were holding their teddy bears and eating popcorn and drinking from huge water bottles that also had guts are were in cheap pyjamas and were holding gummi bears, which some of the PhDs took from their water bottles and threw.

They bounced all over the place.

"Where's Manfred?" asked Lemuel.

"He's still in hospital," said Forrest Deacon, "he's going to do a live stream."

"If only they'd asked," I said, "and they would have gotten living water from the one who makes well."

And Manfred appeared on the big screen.

He was behind a grey tarpaulin, like the sort you have for school photographs, and he was smiling. His curls, which had been a wig that I'd found in Torres Strait on my vacation, were now replaced by a beehive do as blonde as a chevy.

"Hello," said Manfred, "I'm just going to wait for everyone to come online. Okay, hello Google, hello Julian Assange, hello Gab.ai's AI, hello Norton Antivirus, hello Patrick Curlewis."

"Busted," said Forrest, and facepalmed.

"Mannie," I whined, "how many times do we have to do this?"

Epilogue:

17th January 2020

So we're in Ghana which has been spliced by some cuckoo variation of quantum entanglement to Allentown, Bethlehem, Bedlam, Telethis, and Seaford, Victoria, Australia.

Fiona has had her hair done into ringlets, and they've put a visual app on her to give her dimples on film. I'm not sure that was anything more than superfluous.

"The whole world's watching," I said, "no pressure."

I gave her the thumbs up. Fiona gave one back and stuck out her tongue.

"And action," said Lemuel.

And Fiona sang this song:

So we are loved

All the little children are cared for

All the babies in their beds

Are dreaming

And their dreaming of the time

When they will stand in line

And be princes and princesses

But NOW is their time

She giggled.

Because Jesus loves the children

He puts us on the sofa

"Sofa, little children." is what he says

And we rest in our sofa beds

And we listen to stories

About all the big bible things

In the big big bible

That is so very good

"She forgot all about the stuff she wanted this movie to be," I said to Leah, quietly, offset.

"No," said Leah, "she just drafted it in her head."

She smiled at me with that marvellous face.

"It's allowed, Paddy."

And she put her hand high on my shoulder.

"What do you think we're going to do after this?" I asked her. "Like, what happened after Manfred's conference of paranoia is dwarfed compared to this. This is so beautiful, so pure, like it's like heaven. Again, it's like heaven. I thought a knew what heaven was, but this goes beyond what I could have even asked or thought."

"Think again," said Leah, "and God will go deep and exceedingly deeper."

And Jesus Christ looked from Heaven, at the right hand of his father. And he wrote a million poems to Fiona Melanie Grae Curlewis. Just for her. In all the ways that He loved her so, so, so, so, so much. More than I ever could.

God bless you, my child.

And God bless you, everyone at home.

It's only about you if it leads you to eternal life, because that's the voice of Jesus.

Turn away from paranoia. So what if everyone can hear you?

Turn away from sin. A wicked and adulterous generation demands a sin.

Fiona wants to say something to you.

Yeah, you.

"Hello, are you feeling a bit sad? Did you hear a bad song on the radio about a breakup or cheating and it made you mad because you thought it was being your soundtrack for your judgement day movie? Did you look in a newspaper and think it was talking about you?

But they're not talking about you, silly.

I'm talking about you.

Right now.

Jesus loves you so, so, so, so, much. He is so big, so strong and so mighty, there's nothing he can't do for you.

You believe in the cross and you'll be saved, and you'll be with all the real people, not the reel people. Daddy says that a reel is where they held the abba log film in the 1970s. Must have been filming princesses waltzing!

And you'll be okay. You can dream sometimes, but the dreams won't take over. They will help you make life better. You can shut the window and go out and play, or be with a friend who is lonely. Maybe he's on ice, maybe she's protesting weather.

Maybe they're your sweetheart and YOU DON'T EVEN KNOW IT YET.

Thank you for reading this Sand Partridge story. Love Fiona Curlewis, royal cycle Patrick Princess. xx amen

17th January 2020

12:42AM

Saint Patrick And The Call A Jane Injection

20th January 2020
12:03PM
Rot Rage
20th January 2019
Finished 2:55PM

Patrick Curlewis was sitting in a giant toybox in Lemuel Goldstein's latest blockbuster. It was called *Goy Storage*, and was about a reverse Adolf Hitler who only killed Gentiles, straights and normal Christians who were medically perfect.

I was dressed with plantinum blonde hair, blue eyes and duck feathers with a crimson jumpsuit. And I was pale.

Leah Arena walked in, and she was olive skinned with crimpy, curly long black hair like a gypsy and a very genuine face, not her own face, but a face that didn't hide anything and from whom you could hide nothing.

She was wearing a pair of pink, yellow and purple angel wings, which were very fluffy and made of albatross and shrimp feathers. She also had a boa the colour of a Rabbi's tallitot.

"Hey, baby," I said, "I won't harass your scarf, because you Jews are in charge."

"Wake me up on judgement day, hun," she said, "now, let's dance."

"Well, I basically have to do whatever you tell me." I said.

"That's what love means," said Leah.

And she popped Fatboy Slim's Praise You into the CD player. And we danced. I was like Ian Anderson meets Puck from

Shakespeare and she was jittering like Ginsberg's jelly roll from one of his songs.

"Where did you get those scars on your wrists?"

"Oh these?" said Leah, pointing to the pink fills that crossed her, "I was wounded in the house of my friends."

"Yeah?"

"In Bethlehem," she said.

"Oh really?"

"So you're friends with Freud?"

"We are in Germany, baby, everyone who loves the Jews is a Freud."

"Watch what you say, they'll be calling you a radical."

"Just need to add some thunder, baby."

And then my daughters in law Emily, Anne and Charlotte Curlewis came in and started dancing too like they were Denise Drysdale.

"We are tennants in a whiffy hall," I said, "who let off some steam?"

"It was me," said Charlotte, "I love to talk and talk and talk. I can be very blunt, but that's what steam is like, you know?"

"And I thought you had such lovely airs, Charlotte."

She smiled at me, all lip gloss and raver delight.

"Actually, I'm Jane, Jane Eastern!"

"Cut!"

I was losing my cool, and I drank a cup of lukewarm coffee on the dresser to try and heat up. When you're being persecuted for your faith by a reverse Adolf Hitler you need any heat you can get. I swallowed, because I am not Jesus. I am his servant. Worship God and not me!

Forrest Deacon came up, and he was livid.

"BOW DOWN BEFORE ME!" he bellowed. "Jane! What are you doing as Patrick's daughter? Don't you know he's going to have to be patient more if you keep messing with his head!"

"I'm sorry," Jane said, shapeshifting back into my twin sister from Parahrabah, "I just like hanging around my brother."

Lenny Mettle walked up, bringing us croissants that looked like danish.

"Double agent pastry," he said.

"Protestant or Catholic?" I asked.

"Spirit filled," I said, "which is a bit unorthodox."

"Though mine tastes like vodka," says Jane, taking a bite.

"Great Australian taste," I said, "mine's like a song in the dead of night."

"Don't be a weasel," said Anne, "that's really bad taste."

Forrest lifted his finger.

"We mustn't be derivative," he said, "not yet, but we must educated the masses on the horrors of the holocaust. Like, it's not funny at all. It's not funny at all when people die and are humiliated. We should raise people like that from the dead and let them hug a really close friend after they have made up with their Dad."

We all bowed our heads, sober as a cliff of Dover, and we had Lemuel Goldstein began to read a verse , and he read it in an English accent, a bit like that lovely character from The Book Place.

Der HERR ist mein Licht und mein Heil;

vom wem sollte ich mich fürchten?

Chapter 2

Rerachelling

20th January 2020

Hello, we get back to our story. Yes, Patrick has had his fun, hasn't he? He has been a fool. And sometimes you need to be a fool, especially when talking to Corinithians, who are as thick as a chocolate wafer and just as candid. We see him listeing his lists, which is like listing, but it's a bit more ecstatic. So we see he reads his Torah, and he listens to the wind. And he eats a thousand pieces of chocolate, and he hides, and he waits for Rachel Circus to get out of one of her turns. But she has turned into the lady with the ringlets and the olive skin. She has renamed her name, she has faced an old name, and repented of her waywardness. She has danced the dance with Patrick, and so whatever version of Leah that he gets, he can accept her, and merely change genres in the dance. And when you dance with ants in the pants, you cannot consider your ways, because you cannot see what is bothering you. And that is a lazy way of dealing with relationships. So Jew and all that have opposed them: it is sad, it mortification, it bad, it so bad that grammar gets worms. And when the church is divided, that's for Dad to do. He divides, not that the body fights war on itself, that it needs AIDS in the way of royal commissions, but that it has its organs to make the music of life.

My children, love one another as Jesus have loved you. And you say, how has he loved me? He has put me through hell. He has put me in the toybox, in the psych ward with sensory sea snakes and chocolate buttons. I do not like it. That's what you say.

But, God is above this, God is above theatre. Remember Blaise Pascal in his famous Pensees, those fragments sewn into his soft clothing. He said, that uniform is what creates the illusion of rank. Don't picture them in their underwear, but maybe put them in something more palpable for the palate. Put them in a costume, put them as a famous archaeologist. Put them as an alien with a Quarter Stein of apple juice looking for King Solomon's Ursa Major, because that was a bigger deal than gold, which all of the aliens were looking for on Earth, and ended up abducting Grubby and Dee Dee from Gold 104.3. Think of them as Ludwig Othello reading you scripture through the lens of an Estonian banker with an interest in idling his car while reading a Hindi translation of Schindler's Ark. Think of them as a winsome cab driver harmonising to himself using the radiation of Chernobyl captured through the X-Files episode about the forest that ran so much there was a genuine explosion. I think it was directed by Robert Zemeckis, or was that one where Steffany Mackintosh was a plumber eating cake in the basement?

And here is the beauty and truth of the subject, the conscuption of the indubition:

Life, o life, o life. Let's have new life after the division, and we'll hug a lot after the pain passes, baby.

20th January 2020
3:22PM

Saint Patrick

Apostate Bursters

20th-21st January 2020

Dedicated to Jesus Christ;

Who means what he says,

Names names,

And changes them round!

Special thanks to Dean Woodward

Chapter 1:

The Crusty Old Case Of Swedenborg Roberts Robot

20th-21st January 2020 (11:57PM, 20th)

"Love is beautiful, don't you think love is beautiful. A lot of peeps don't think love is beautiful, their heart is walking in innocence, and it knows, the brain is seeking the next calculation, and this station is a nation of beautiful lovely people. Look at this: look what's streaming after this read season."

At the beach in Malibu, there is a blonde haired lady who looks a lot like Jane Eastern. Her hair is braided, and she looks a lot like a dutch girl, you know, who carries two pails of milk on a stick.

I don't know art, but I don't read into it things I shouldn't.

And this lady is smiling and people ask her things and they get the answer. People ask for a gypsy reading, and she plays them a photoshopped montage of gravy tea.

"What's your name, sweetheart?" said Trooper O'Donahugh, who was a man in a fedora hat and looked like he had been eating risotto and hadn't wiped his face.

"Hello, 17308," she said, "my name is 160270-328560=328, but you Americans can call me Swedenborg Roberts the Robot."

Trooper O'Donahugh shook her hand.

"Ooh," he said, "you're so cold. You don't hang round with the other girls, do you?"

"I am here to tell you about my wedneslet wena hg wi." she said.

"That sounds marvellous," said Trooper.

"Let me tell you the truth," said Swedenborg, "the truth is that you've got it all wrong. This isn't really Malibu. It's a place for us in the meadow where the duck agents of space rat fancy manifest their donf, ijsdnfngouhdfgl sldf lsig msndif ln."

"Wow, that really speaks to me," said Trooper, "where do you meet with your friends? I'd love to come and listen to you rap a bit."

"Why that is easy," said Swedenborg, "we don't meet, we teem, and we don't have friends, we have reso mwoegh uegli. See, our reso mwoegh uegli teem every Sunday, which we call Sportigum the Twenty First."

"Yes," Trooper said, "these liars have corrupted the world, haven't they? We've got what they need."

"I'm glad you see things my way fjju mosif nuhsdfg idli glisdf glidsng lianl gi," said Swedenborg.

So fjju mosif nuhsdfg idli glisdf glidsng lianl gi went and was very happy.

But Swedenborg Roberts Robert was a Gogloid, that is, an AI of great magnitude sent by Gog. Manfred Eastern was still in hospital with his head injury of 1000 times megalomania (pardon my Dutch math).

And she smiled the smile of a thousand dances.

A boy was in Malibu drinking a glass of Cea, he merged perfectly with the VW beetles.

It was Allen N Curlewis, and he was 12 years old. He was a bit sickly, and a bit of a dreamer, but he wanted to get some rays. His father Patrick really tried to get him healthy, and they'd go to church every Sunday and pray over him and go through Fire Tunnels where everyone would pray for you and you'd feel like some kind of super Bar Mitzvah wedding rugby match book of Proverbs meets Sirach meets Holy Ghost throwing streamers of light coloured puff of great significance.

That's how Allan N Curlewis saw it.

He was taking a lot of saw palmetto, and his hair was quite thick now. It was easier to get Saw Palmetto in California than Australia. When he was in Australia, he'd use Vegemite.

Because that's what Americans reckon they do, and when in Australia do as the Americans think Australians do. Right?

So Allen saw Swedenborg Roberts the Robot, and he broke into song:

"Oh black shuck, black duck, bluck run of the mill. Blue eyed beige coloured bonce of buco, bystanders of beligerent bentheian bystanders, and broke bolders of biance. And I love my mum and I love my Dad. My Dad is beautiful, a beautiful man. He likes to dress up, and he likes to wear what he can to wear down the apostates. An apostate is someone who tries to make you say sorry which is supposed to free you, but that gives you no permission anymore to be free, but to do what they say. A fundamentalist can be an apostate. An apostate can be a blue buried buos. Bji ufgmodfsinhnlsi fg.

And so it goes, my cyborg, friend? Are you my friend? Do you feet my shop? Do you fot my doam. What is your name, monica? Or Augustine, thou art my spm ,/, and I see a field of mer; and I am a fountain of blue. And I love you, Julie Andrews. So very, very much. And Jesus wants to marry you in Heaven. Don't give up, you don't have nine, got to be so very fine but do not do anything but be sane. Love Allen."

And Swedenborg Roberts the Robot...

She cried real tears, and decided that she wanted to be a painter.

***

Meanwhile, in his lair, Manfred Eastern screwed up another blueprint.

"Curse that Allen N. Curlewis!" he said, "That was my 144,000th false prophet!"

Amen.

Catholic Bugs Invade Murdochland

22nd - 23rd January 2020

This is dedicated to Bradley Kuipers.

My first friend at Bayside Christian College.

Prologue:

Love Is Like Good News To Stuffed Animals
OR
Supertramp Is Zone 3
22nd January 2020
Finished 6:04PM

I was very thirsty on the set of my new movie, filmed in Murdochland, by the Baxter Railway station. I drank a chinotto, and then another, and then another, and people were staring at me wishing I would stop.

I opened the door and understood the darkness in there held an old vulpine fur, with one blue eye and one green eye. I regretted that such a thing had happened, and I took the fox furry down.

"Do you know the good news, little fox?" I said. "Jesus loves you."

And the fox lived to see another day, and ran out into Somerville where it went into space at Eramosa Road.

Love is a beautiful thing, love is a holy thing, love is a pure thing. Love is noble and true and beautiful and lively and destined to be a thing that grows richer and richer day by day.

I was getting desperate, and I knew I could do this scene anyway I wanted. All this drinking of soft drinks had really judged my molars, and I wriggled a loose tooth.

"I'm getting too old for this," I said, "nurse!"

And Leah Curlewis came to me, with a crown of fifty dollar bills and a filling.

"There," she said, "each tooth has its twin, not one is missing."

"Darling," I said, "that's a bit raw in public."

Chapter 1

Mer-Ravers And Catholic Bugs

22nd January 2020

The movie was me playing Yeshua and Jodie Tulk playing Mary Magdalene. Jodie Tulk is not Leah at all. Jodie Tulk is a friend of Jesus whom he liked to talk to.

I am dressed in white, with brown hair like a son of Mrs Robinson.

My phone rings. It's my mother, Monaghan P. Curlewis.

"Hello, Pat. I'm so glad you're leaving a legacy for your kids."

"Well, you have to feed an army," I said.

"Generally, you do," said Mum.

"I think I drank too much pop," I said.

"Your Dad can hear you," said Mum, "he's on the loudspeaker."

Wednesdaddio Albert Pointer Quackeire Cor De Noms Curlewis yelled something.

"How are ya, buddy?"

"I'm at Baxter," I said.

"That's great. Did you know that's Taxer B when you shift the letters?"

"Who Taxer B?" I said.

"Are you forgetting your nanna's birthday?" said Wednesdaddio Albert Pointer Quackeire Cor De Noms Curlewis.

Taxer B Curlewis was my grandmother, and she was Catholic. She was the most Catholic Catholic that ever lived. She was so Catholic that she even thought like a Catholic.

"Well, I could come and see her after we should the film." I said.

"He says he can come round after he should," said Dad to someone in a recorded room on the end of the phone.

I rolled my eyes.

"Nothing is just rubbish," I said, looking at all the empty chinotto cans. "Maybe I could cut them in two and grow some alfalfa in them."

"Are you going to do that right this instant, Paddy?" said my director, who was called Phantom Custard.

"Hi Phan," I said, "I suppose I could grow some rice too, but yeah I can wait before I start propagating."

"Okay, let's do this picture," said Phantom, and the acts were spoken into being; miracle of it all.

I completely forgotten to mention what the Mer-Ravers and Catholic Bugs were.

Chapter 2

Wednesdaddio Albert Pointer Quackeire Cor De Noms Curlewis Rings

22nd-23rd January 2020

So me and Jodie are playing Jesus and Mary. Here we are. And we recap. I wear a chef's hat, and Jodie wears a Davy Crockett one.

Phantom Custard says:

"And *Jesus is Groovy And Also Lit*, take One."

And we go walking into the Baxter shops, to the Woolworths.

"This is where the Lamb goes," I said.

Let's get into character and use Biblical names, this is how it goes:

"Are you a vegan, Jesus?" asked Mary Magdalene.

"Love is split when a lamb dies, and when a man dies, he offers himself to the wall. I am the wall, if you are willing to receive it, and I am the door in the wall if you are willing to enter. I am the way, but also the mercy of the blessed one. I am ever present and so helpful to you. So Mary Christmas, let's go and get some Maxibons and carrots, and then get a 75 cent litre bottle of tonic and some sakatas and we'll go down to the underpass, and we'll have legitimate fire and ask the Father for a chance that you get married to someone."

"And cut." said Director Custard.

Chapter 3

Motorcycle Roller

23rd January 2020

Me and Leah are riding a bike down the bike tracks, we are at an undisclosed location high in the Santa Monica Mountains.

"I think we need some better stuff in our fridge," said Leah, "you drink chinotto all the time; and you are always ringing people from other countries! The phone bill is so thoroughly abstract it's painting me red!"

"Well better than whitewashing the truth," I said.

"Patrick, you need to eat better," she said, "you can't just eat chips. You're so habitual it's not even a surprise when you make the choices you make. And I love surprises, Patrick. I love them so much. I love when you are with me. I love listening to you and talking to you. As long as you don't have a foul mouth either and stand up to the devil."

"I've stood up to Manfred Eastern so many times I need an abacus," I said.

"No, Patrick," said Leah, "the devil. I'm glad you don't know him, but just know that there are such things. That's not something to be stoked about, okay?"

We parked the car, and there was a sign at the corner store in the Santa Monica Mountains.

And the headline read.

"Liar is Not For You."

"Oh, man!" I said.

"Oh, man!" Leah said.

Leah started trembling, and her hand was all wriggly. I held it until my wrist wriggled a bit and then we were calm.

"I'm so sorry, love," I said, "I guess having a new job was something I'd been looking forward to for a while. I don't want to misrepresent Jesus or put words in his mouth. Though I am very experimental and Ziontific, in my heart of hearts I'd really like to be a fun-literalist. I don't want to forget who my LORD is. I don't want to forget the Father gave me your precious, precious heart. Oh my God, Leah, I am so devastated that I've been so sloppy."

"Don't let the antichrist blunt your resolve," said Leah, smiling like a giggle that was telepathic medicine, "come on. We don't read into things if we don't have to. It's not kosher. And you as a psychiatrist know that. Resist the devil and he will flee from you."

I stopped and thought about this. I thought I saw something out of the corner of my eye but nobody believes me.

"Legally," I said, "legally, do Manfred and Jane have to co-parent baby London?"

"He's not a baby," said Leah, "he's a big boy."

"Great," I said, "it's good to have milestones as long as you don't move them into black water."

"I despire myself for watch the black woods of the mergatroid." said Leah.

"What you are is a wreath of a thousand backward burgundy inception weasels." I said.

"Would you give me the time of your red wood inception butter rancid witch bell fury agrus manfred like plouter." said Leah.

And then I stopped.

In that moment, we had been taken to hell.

Chapter 4

Wiggle Wiggle Wiggle Oculum O'Faerre

23rd January 2020

We were burning in hell.

And there was a tall, blanched, blonde man with soft features. And he was wearing ivory and had a single orchid in his lapel, and the delicate parts were half scrunched into the pockets with a lining of the substance of a glasses case, soft and beige.

"Boo yah!" he said, "Hello Putfarge! And Errol Vininia! I am Wiggle Wiggle Wiggle Oculum O'Faerre, but you can call me FERICUL!"

"I will never call you Groovy," I spat, "even if I burn for it!"

There was silence for about 43 days.

And then we left hell and we were back in Croydon.

"What was that, Patrick?" said Leah, leaning on my shoulder.

"I don't know," I said, "I think we need help with our relationship."

She held me and we sat on a park bench.

"Patrick," she said, kind of pleading but so warm and so nice that you would have said yes to absolutely anything that followed, "our children need us to be one in everything. We can't be slack and do stupid stuff."

"When do you ever do stupid stuff?" I asked, leaning back from our hug, but because I wanted to be closer to her thoughts.

I needed to see her distant that I may see the whole of her.

"Patrick," she said, "I feel guilty when I don't parent the kids right. Like Fiona, she asked me for a shepherd's dress because she wanted to be little bo peep. And I said I would, and I went to the Ritchies in Mornington to go get it, and I don't think I told the truth, because I didn't keep my promise. And she was really upset and threw her custard at me."

"Sounds heavy," I said, not trying to sound stupid.

"And I was guilty about that *all* week, Paddy," she said, "I mean, it doesn't show on my face, any of my faces, but in my One Heart it does. I really want to be a Perfect Mother, Patrick."

I rested my hand on her shoulder, kind of reaching across from her left to her right, so it kind of crossed her heart.

"I hope I can live demonstratably, righteously; eternally avascilatingly, to be your counsellor, my lovey dovey," I said, "and I know that's a bit awkward, my language, because this is like heart stuff, and the heart is a bit F. R. David on Top of the Pops."

"You've got good direction, Paddy," said Leah, "you're so good at staying on the path. Yes, you've been nutty, but that happens in marriage, even with all the responsibilities."

"Please let me be sane to you, Leah O'Curlewis."

"Please, let me explain with gentleness, Padthick."

"Ha!"

She nestled into me and we watched the traffic for a while. Melbourne traffic is unique, but that's not the point.

Chapter 5
Jane And The Gymnasts

23rd January 2020

   Jane Eastern and Manfred Eastern were taking London Eastern down to Wilson's Promontory. REM's Orange Crush was playing as they went through the windy bits of sea and mountain and forest and sand and cliff and God looking into a mirror.

Chapter 6

Oh, I Forgot The Gymnasts

23rd January 2020

In the psych ward known as Twin America Honest Alcatraz to the astute patients, Jane was on nursing duty. Only one of her was with Manfred. She really didn't want to be there, and she kept this to herself.

The public phone was scarred like a twin's side after psychology. And there was a man named Beligerent Bithrani writing math all over the patients rights and responsibilities.

"Are you okay?" said Jane, but with trepidation because she didn't want to be hurt. She kept her distance distant.

Beli laughed.

"Swim if you can in my paptism of Catholic hoy, sin sauce. Oips. Whe, diuhg udng bkaignbdlifngailbsnfug lnusdgliausfgoasfgo;uafuxliughljkgcidn fluigdmgf ."

"Are you Charismatic Catholic?" asked Jane gently, gently touching Beli's elbow.

"Am I?" he said.

"What do you want for yourself, Beli."

"I want Real Food," said Beli and started to cry, clutching on Jane and shuddering like he was being electocuted.

"Oh my gosh," said Jane, "um... we can get you some tapioca? Or some rice pudding?"

"Do you have gello?" he asked.

"Oh, I'm pretty close to the gello," said Jane, "it's in the kitchen by the nurses station."

"Could you train me in how to make it?" asked Beli.

"You don't need me," said Jane, taking Beli's hand and leading him to the kitchen, "but I can guide you through it. I'll stand behind you and give you directions."

"Oh... ok," said Beli.

They reached under the bench to the bottom shelf and produced a packet of Aeroplane Jelly. It was green. Whatever flavour that is. I'm not sure, probably tastes like Dr Pepper.

"I'm trapped here, aren't I?" said Beli.

"Do you know why you're here?" she asked.

"I just wanted to see you," he said.

"Oh Beligerent," said Jane, "that's inappropriate."

"Yeah," said Beli, "but I thought robbing a milk bar of all the snickers bars was pretty gutsy myself."

"They're even worse when they're fried," said Jane, "come on, put the crystals into the plate."

"Pretty," said Beli, as they all fell in.

They looked like sands that blazed a continuum of hues.

"Algebraic," he said.

"Now add up how many cups of hot water you need."

"How come it needs to be hot?" Beli asked.

"Sums like it hot," said Jane, "that's what chemistry means."

"Something doesn't add up," said Beli.

"Paddle the mix with your spoon," said Jane.

"It's all solving, but I must remember I got a D." said Beli.

"We all have trouble sometimes with our work," said Jane, rolling her eyes.

"Ace!" said Beli, "it's like a Monster Drink!"

"No Monsters in the psych ward!" said Jane, and slapped Beli on the side.

"I know," said Beli, pouting, "it's never okay. The paramedics need the wake up, not the ones in the stretcher."

"I'm not protesting with that sentiment," said Jane.

"And then we put it on ice?" asked Beli.

"No Ice!" said Jane, and belted him over the head with an ironing board, "No, we just leave it on the shelf."

"Death of a party," said Beli, and fainted as the jelly settled.

And Jane faded out, as if life was paused like a bear with a fish.

Whoever she is.

Chapter 7

A Song For The Sower Seed, Tell You What?

Live

Don't be afraid

Live

Don't be afraid

Look up

Look up

Do you see the light

The globes

They are all over her

All over the Earth

All over

Streetlights that glow even brighter

In brownouts

And there is no stoner

When the evangelist

Sings of darkness

And the light shines on

And live, live, live

I know that on the surface

It is do do do

And you are overworked and dirty

And flushed

But know that you will be clean

Othniel Poole

You will be okay,
You will be so okay
So knock out the evil
And turn it upside down
Get all the good out of the bad
The diamonds from the rough
The lalala's from the Shangri Las
The new men from the psych doc cars

1:11PM
And I love you
I love you patient one
I love so
So

One of the frames of mind of
The antichrisT seemed
To have been erased
But he had
Made a full recovery

- Revelation 13:3 (Patrick Curlewis Paraphrase)
You would dare paraphrase God?
- Chuck Missler, founder of Koinonia House

You Are Beautiful, Blue Eyed Patrick

A St Patrick Story

Contents:

1: Green And Gold Mogen Rock And Prog

2: Eastern Freeway

3: Blessed Are The Poor, For They Are Animals

4: Morris Got Courage

5: ?

1: Green And Gold Mogen Rock And Prog

24th January 2020

Manfred Eastern burst from the double doors of the psych ward and into the Monash University trainee nurses station.

"Hello ladies," he said, "do you believe in God?"

And they looked at him and kind of smiled, but were very considerate, indeed.

"Will you come with us, Manfred?"

"Oh, that's cold," he said, "and you may think I'm lukewarm but I know Cold! Did you know my wife was from Siberia? Well, now she's an android, the 144,001st one."

"Here's your phone back, Mr Eastern," she said, "you've got the answer you want, you're free to leave Twin America Honest Alcatraz and go back to being leader of the Wally Dirt Orb."

"Where's that?" said Manfred.

"Planet A," they said, "there is no Planet B."

"Then where did all the Bees go?" asked Manfred.

"I think Andy Warhol stole them," said a blonde nurse, and they all started laughing.

"You know, you paint me out to be a fool," said Manfred, "but I rule over you, bow down before me."

"Oh behave, Mannie," said a male nurse with brown hair.

And they gave him his perscription, which was a copy of Anna Karenina and a bottle of gobstoppers which had the winning raffle ticket for numbering them all.

"Oh boy," said Mannie, "well, do I eat the gobstoppers? How many do I eat a day?"

"Oh, you're pretty messed up, but we can visit you in social visits," said a lady.

"I'd love to have you home with me," said Manfred to the lady, "but I do love my devices and my son Lon."

He then burst through the doors of the hospital and walked down the road to the Catholic Church.

He split open his cheap hospital pyjamas; and shining out more than a hero was a star of David in gold on a backing of green.

He shed his skin, and was dressed in all green with the star of gold big and saffron over his chest.

"Join me, lovers of my soul," he said.

2: Eastern Freeway

24th January 2020

It was Easter, and Jane Eastern was giving away Candy Canes at the JB-Hi-Fi at Chapel Street, South Yarra.

"You're a bit out of place," said a man with a cross earring.

"I know you're not a comrade, sir," she said.

"That's right, sweetheart," he said, "I'm Jupiter, Jupiter Merigan."

"Pleased to meet you, darling," said Jane.

"Spose you want to go astral travelling?" he said.

"I am not new age," she said, "I am Orthodox Chrisitan."

"Oh, but even they have to submit to the UN."

"We are struggling with God, we communists," said Jane, "and as you know, the Chosen Ones will reign."

"Oh, man," said Mr Merigan, "plagues of dogs and cats couldn't get me to go back to Tennesee and all the drunken wisdom."

"Yes, it is much more peaceful here," said Jane.

"Do you drink, Mrs Jane Eastern?"

"I drink water," she said, "but not only water, I must drink red and be well read because I am Orthodox Christian."

"I suppose you have a lot of apps on your phone, being a spy," said Jupiter, and reached for Jane's trenchcoat.

"Don't touch the merchandise, you player!" she said, "I can shout you a pot if you want. But I'm not going to marry you, for the sake of My Lord."

"Well a pot's a pot," said Jupiter, "do you know the best bar in Chapel Street?"

"It's always changing," said Jane, "I know better when I get home and go on the web."

"I like webcrawler," said Jupiter, "I am a browser hipster."

"That's what JB-Hi-Fi means, Jupit," said Jane.

"Don't get my down, love." said Mr Merigan.

"Well, do I mime for a cab and we can go to bar?"

"Well I'd rather use Chrome first," said Merigan.

"Get your own phone, comrade," said Jane.

"Well don't you socialist's share?" asked Merigan.

"Yes," said Jane, "but we also have an angry button."

"Yes, I've seen it," said Jupiter, "it is a big red spot."

"Speak for yourself," said Jane, "you are just copying lines you see on TV."

"Well you socialists also are obsessed with subtitles."

"It is hard to speak the language of the heart, comrade."

"Are we going to drink or what?"

"We can eat too, comrade, I am very friendly. I am the friendliest girl in the West."

"But you're Eastern, Jane."

"Exactly," she said, "now let's have a great Friday and like Jesus, not get plastered, but... er... I'm sorry, I want to be Orthodox Christian."

"That's what faithfulness means," said Jupiter, crossing his arms and rolling his eyes.

3: Blessed Are The Paw, For They Are Animals

24th January 2020

At the vet, Leah was looking after bandana birds. That is to say, a bird like a kestrel or a dove, that has been dressed to look like a pirate.

"R is for Russia," said Leah, "so when you see a Russian invading, what do you say, Charlie?"

"Arrrrrr," said Charlie the kestrel.

"Arrrr," said Leah.

"Arrrr," said Charlie.

Leah rattled the cage.

"Arrr," said Leah.

She sat down and saw that she was handcuffed to the chair.

"Oh yeah," she said, "Manfred has locked me up at this vet. Is the war over? Has the Man of Sin really won?"

Manfred entered with a crown of fifty dollar bills and the jar of gobstoppers.

"Bubula Western," she said.

Who said?

4: Morris Got Courage

24th January 2020

Morris Mettle was at South Yarra station, out the front, preaching by the tram lines.

Patrick Curlewis was there too, handing out vitamin C pills to pur'e the common cold.

"If you have ever told a lie," said Morris, "you are a sinner in danger of hell. If you have ever stolen, you are in danger of Gehenna. If you have ripped up a Bible, the Bible says that..."

Jupiter Merigan and Jane Eastern were walking up the hill from Chapel Street, each with a glass of rose in their hands, in very bombastic fiddly wine glasses that looked like they could have been from Captain Cook's ship, or an episode of Jim Henson.

"Hey," said Jupiter, " Bible means book, right?"

Morris, who was now used to interruptions, looked down and smiled.

"Yeah, it does," he said, "it's the Holy Book. The Word of God. The Spirit Filled 66."

"Well, I just got a parking ticket," said Jupiter, producing the receipt, "I was booked, and so I was Bibled, and I'd love to rip it up, but I'm bugged that I can't and have to pay the price."

"Well, Jesus paid the price for my sins and yours," said Morris.

"So you'll pay for my parking ticket?" said Ju.

Patrick took the receipt off the Chapel man and studied it.

"It's not too much, Mozza," he said, "it's about $2.50."

"I spent all my money on pretzels," said Jupiter, "Jane loves German food."

"Like her or not," said Mr Mettle, "if you can't pay, it's like you owed a billion dollars."

"But it's easier to get $2.50 off a hobo than a billion off a CEO." said Jupiter.

"You can have your idols," said Morris, "but you need Jesus Christ."

"So you could give me $2.50?"

"Give to everyone who asks, Mozza," Patrick grated, "that's Jesus' words."

Morris sighed and took out his wallet, but it was stuck tight in his pants because he hadn't used it in a while, and when he pulled with gusto, it came out and smacked Patrick Curlewis in the head.

Patrick passed out on the pavement.

"Oh Esau's shoulder fuzz!" said Jane, "Paddy!"

And Morris and Jupiter tried to make him comfortable. Jupiter pocketed the money with his other hand.

"He needs to breathe," said Jane, taking a breath, "I'm going to try to resurrect him."

Jupiter took a laser pointer and pointed to Patrick's mouth.

"You put your mouth here, sweetie," he said.

"Please don't be absurd, Jupit," said Jane and slapped Mr Merigan on the shoulder.

Mr Merigan shrugged and drank a sip of wine.

Jane gave Patrick a kiss that burned.

"Oh," cried Patrick, "oh, I am so stoned!"

He got up, bleary eyed and full of tears.

"Righteousness and peace," said Jupiter, "I have just seen that now, what rel'gion are you lot?"

"We're Fun-Literalist Christians," said Patrick, "I'm a psychiatrist, and Jane is a nurse and actress, and I'm also an actor, and Morris is a delicatessen and a street preacher, and he does make a good gnocchi, says my daughter Fiona."

"Well, I think I might like to join you," said Jupiter.

Patrick shook his hand.

"Always good to have a helicopter convert," he said, "the Father draws those he loves to Himself."

"Artistic," said Mr Merigan.

5: ?

24th January 2020

Love is partient, that is, a piece of the peace of a ward with a man who listenes when he speaks, and he procures the method of a thousand holy dreams and enters the plague like a vaccination of holiness, blessed by the Lord and what he has brought unto the method shepherds of insitgrated water, and how we go is how ewe goes. And how the people dance and they sing a million years full of drinks and blessing so beautiful and wise. And bless you greatest planet, like a sun, like a sun. Welcome to the Kingdom, Oh J. Merigan!

2:09PM

24th January 2020

Kahlua And Robinson

A Saint Patrick Romance

25th January 2020

Contents:

One: The Blessing

Two: Anchovy Benjimite

Three: Anne Clicks Okay And All Hearts Shown Well To Do! Selah; S'rach L; Amen'

Five: Kylma Tadblake

One: The Blessing:

25th January 2020

Anne Eastern was reading a book of crossword puzzles in an old barber shop. There were golden steins of beer all over the shop, because it was a barber's shoppe, and people were speaking in tongues of faere.

Jupiter Merigan was cutting her hair, but there didn't seem to be any scissors that worked.

"They're all blunt!" said Jupiter, "Oh my daisy, I'm going to have to calm down and get a cheese'burger."

"Watch it," said Heaven Holdenmerry, his assistant, "you don't want that thing going to your heart, it will change your life."

"Oh, my life's already been changed," said Jupiter, "I'm not clowning around; I'm a Fun-Literalist Christian thanks to the avunculism of Pareick;"

Anne sniggered and brought the crossword puzzle closer to her sight.

"What is Evangelism," said Heaven, who heard Jupiter in his own language. Phyrigian or thereabouts. It's all in Acts.

"It's like flying," said Jupiter, "it's like messengers of God going round you and making you feel safe."

"So it's like being at Tiffany's listening to Beck's Odelay?"

"No, we don't cut it like that," said Jupiter, "Come on, Heaven! Come down to Earth! Come down to Earth and meet the Lord Jesus Christ."

"Jesus Christ, you're zealous," said Heaven.

Anne put down the puzzle book.

"You know, honey," said Jupiter, "I don't think you really need a haircut; to be perfectly honest, I think you need a lot more body and a lot more hair."

"I'm a good girl," said Anne, and gave Jupiter a hug and walked out with just a few tips flashing through her locks.

Two: Anchovy Benjimyte;

25th January 2020

Street Evangelist Morris Mettle had invited Patrick Curlewis, psychiatrist and actor, to a power conference at a festival in Haiti.

"Players gotta play," said Allen Nathaniel Curlewis, Patrick's son who was healed as a baby. He was on his Nintendo Switch.

"Are you going to pay attention?" I asked.

"I'll pay about... ten percent." said Allen.

"This preacher's really good," said Morris, "Anchovy Benjimyte is really into sobriety and power and severity,"

"That's good, because the internet connection here is making me count it all joy," said Allen.

Patrick gave Allen a Mintie.

"What time is it?" asked Allen.

"About time you ate that mint for a while," I said.

And the conference started, they were going to worship heaps and heaps and the end with a bit of praise at zenith, but for now we were hearing Anchovy preach.

"We are going to turn the Temple Tables over," he said, "we are going to break on through the other side. We are going to perceive and not grow cold. We are going, too, say: "the church is not for sissies." We are going to say "we are not going to need to say 'Pardon moi Francais?'"

Morris squinted.

"He's not being very straightforward, is he?" he murmured to me.

"Well, you can't love god and mammon," I said.

Anchovy spread his arms wide and tested everyone with a bottle of wine.

"Do not be drink on whine, but be feeling with the sprohad."

"Is he speaking in tongues?" asked Allen, eyes rising from his Switch.

"Ajh mai fria, dmfg whoops bma my jolu and my hola und alm."

I got up.

"I don't need to put up with this. I never asked for Anchovies on the pizza."

Three: Anne Clicks Okay And All Hearts Shown Well To Do! Selah; S'rach L; Amen'

25th January 2020

Anne shifted her appearance; and she looked like Jane Eastern with her trenchcoat.

An 11 year old was waiting there: just a girl, who was Anne's Jane Eastern version doppleganger that was so exact you may need an ambulance to blur it down a bit with some tetracycline; maybe a dash of minties and some chocolate freckles for the muse.

"Ezza Enoschool," said Anne, "I thank you very much that I've been able to use your appearance as Jane Eastern."

"She doesn't even exist," said Ezza, "it was just a fantasy of *me*! Can the modesty, you just wanted to have a squiz at Patrick Curlewis."

"Yeah, you're the real deal, the cast of the cast," said Anne, smiling.

Though truthfully Anne Eastern is much more beautiful than Ezza Enoschool. And looks nothing like her.

"You are a very smart girl, Ezza," said Anne, blushing, "Having created the Changeling Genome from your own hair."

"Well, I just follow Jesus," said Ezza, "simple gospel."

"But God begins in Genesis," said Anne.

"True," said Ezza, "but I like to exit dux and try something more humble."

Patrick Curlewis was going around doing house calls, when he came to Antichrist Manfred Eastern's house. He came with his webster pack for Man of Sin, which was full of strawberry kiss chocolates.

"Manfred," said Patrick, knocking on the door, "Manfred, you haven't had your medication in 40 days, you must be starving because you haven't been having the right ki'd of dessert."

Manfred answered the door.

"Help me, Patrick!" cried Leah Curlewis from her cage. For Manfred had contained this bird in the back of his own flat.

Leah looked exactly like Anne, with a radiant, holy face and beautiful hair. Manfred, being the villain of the piece, had let her down.

So let me talk in first person to the first.

"What the doughnut are you playing at, Eastern!" I said, "Let go of my wife!"

And then Manfred disappeared.

And there was only a cockatiel in the cage; and a thin, yellow hair.

Five: Kylma Tadblake:

25th January 2020

Patrick Curlewis and Anne Eastern are having lunch by a plate factory, there are China plates and Royal Doultons and lots of rubber chickens, because this is a bit of a joke.

"Shopping here is so much fun," said Anne, "like, you could get something for someone's birthday here."

She put her hands together, palm to palm, in prayer.

"You know you look like you're about to do Martial Arts," I said.

"Is there life on Mars?" she said.

And then I am Patrick.

"Oh boy," I face palmed.

"Here are your chicken schnitzels," said the Waiter, who was Merigan D'vane, Jupiter's funnier brother who was a bit of a player.

"Where's the sauce?" I asked. "And the ham?"

"The ham needs a bit of grace," D'vane said.

"Well, we must prayed."

"Then, pray tell, Paddy, what did you pray?"

"I prayed that I know where my true love is,"

"Well, if you want some cheeses we have swiss, brie, and blue vein."

"Please don't mention brie in front of Anne," I whined.

"We've got Jesus inside of us," said Anne.

"Well, that's for starters," said D'vane, "but you must realise that life is like a box of chocolates. You usually get served at the end."

"Where do the children play here?" I asked.

"In the playground of the loving hats," said D'vane, and pointed to a playground where all these kids were in turbans.

"That's fully sick!" I said.

"We should minister to them," said Anne.

"Yes," I said, "but I just wonder..."

"Kids wonder a lot too, Paddy," said Anne, "you'd be good at counting to seven with them and then getting them to have lunch so they can be strong. They won't even need cutlery, they'll just tear up their sandwiches and give them to all their friends, and there will be planty over left."

And then someone say down beside us, full after a meal.

"I need to air out, sis," she said.

"Who are you?" I said.

"My name is Kylma Tadblake," she said, "I'm Ane's sister."

"You never told me you had a sister," I said to Ane.

"I never told you about me," said Ace.

And then an 11 year old walked up to the table and kissed Kylma on the cheek.

"Hi Mom," said Ezza, "all's well that ends well?"

"As I live and breathe," I said, gasping for air, "I think I need some aoili on this schnitzel."

"Atrick," said Ace, and it seemed like she was saying that as most of the week, "A Trick, it's me... Joke."

"Jac Ee A Trens?" I said.

"Do you need Allen's Nintendo Switch?" asked Dace, producing her son's game from under the table, "read my lips, Trick, you know who I am. I look like how I was during Bible study."

"How come I am funding it tricky to perceive?" I asced.

"David," called Kylma, "David!"

And then Ezza's father came along, David Tadblake, and kissed Kylma on the other cheek.

"This is your brother-in-law, Trick," said Dace, and the story is nearly over.

"I am my own brother-in-law?" I said, trying hard to be or not to be dizzy.

"See clearer," said Ender's, "this is no mere parlez, Trick."

"I drank a glass of apple and raspberry," I said, and drank a glass of Shiraz Cabernet, "and then I said to the kinder's wearing the turbines that we're going to go flying very soon."

"Stop talking in Math, you helicopter," said Ezza, "do you want the calming police to finish you off?"

"Well, they end up being set on fire," I said, and drank some more Shriaz.

"Tell us a story, Paddy," said Ezza, "you were always so good at that."

"Do I know you," I said.

"We've conversed," she said, "and you've been very sneaky."

"Well, let's dissect this thing," I said, sobering up, "I see that er... this Lady who... is sitting next to me, hearing me talk... is... er... um... I guess, she's the One, isn't she."

I looked at Ezza.

"And you are the 11, because of your age," I said, "but I want to tell stories and not be stoned. Time travels, but I think I'm more appalled at the idea."

"Holy Ghost high," said the Lady, "there's nothing like it."

"Well, I'd like to graduate and give you a new name," I said.

"Oh, don't start that again!" whined Ezza.

I blew a raspberry at Ezza.

"You smell like a whingeing pom," she said.

"Well, it's been a surprise, all this," I said, facing the Lady again, "But I'd like to tell the truth. When you tell the truth, you are more like Jesus, and are shown heaven."

"This guy's raining on our parade," said a hard faced diner, "we came out to have a quiet meal, and he's make a scene."

The Lady blew the hard faced diner a raspberry, and Merigan D'vane put a pie in his face, full cream with extra dollop, and a VR Snickers.

"I've got a child-like heart too, Trick" said the Lady, "all Christian ladies do."

"So you're quite small?" I said.

"Yes," she said, very soft.

"Thank you for your honesty."

"That's okay, Padre."

"Dr Curlewis," asked a patient who had escaped.

"Do you mind?" I blurted.

The patient sat down. He was 11 years old and he had seated himself opposite Ezza.

"As I was saying," I said, "I have a new name for you. Truthful and Small, Earnest And Like A Kid,"

She giggled.

"Kindness Ophir Tiny," I said, as if saying steak and chips.

And she said,

"Corban Q .Wedbloom!"

And a revolution of sorcerers couldn't tear us apart.

For what is a magi, a wise man, but of the heart?

1:11PM

25th January 2020

Letters of Tabula and *Saint Patrick* are two books in one, both reflecting family life in perplexing, adventurous environments.

Letters of Tabula alternates between poetry and short stories in the manner of Othniel Poole's poetry volumes, including *Chapel of Green Stone*. It's crowned with the further adventures of the Rosas and the Batistes, both before and after Poole's novel *Gohm*. These include Darcee and Tabula's toddler days involving some strange fruit, bad dreams, and a first reading experience. It also looks to the future, where Tabula and Gohm are married and yet to conceive, and Darcee has yet to find someone.

Saint Patrick features thirteen short stories that continue the adventures of Patrick and Leah Curlewis. He's a supernatural psychiatrist and an actor. The stories follow his adventures in Hollywood and Melbourne, Australia, and all the movie lots and psych wards in between. Therein lies romance, family, and the challenges of relationships. Plus there's a boatload of Dad jokes.

***

Othniel Poole grew up near Melbourne, Australia, and now resides in its suburbs. This is his 13th book, which brings "old characters into the poems, and characters from different places meeting each other. Church history inspired a lot of it, and all the mysteries that are still to be solved, as well as the patterns one is pursued by."

Lightning Source UK Ltd.
Milton Keynes UK
UKHW011318160820
368300UK00001B/22